Other Works by
Jan C

Writing as

MAY MCGOLDRICK

JAN COFFEY AND NIK JAMES

MAY McGOLDRICK NOVELS

A Midsummer Wedding

The Thistle and the Rose

Angel of Skye (Macpherson Trilogy Book 1)

Heart of Gold (Book 2)

Beauty of the Mist (Book 3)

Macpherson Trilogy (Box Set)

The Intended

Flame

Tess and the Highlander

The Dreamer (Highland Treasure Trilogy Book 1)

The Enchantress (Book 2)

The Firebrand (Book 3)

Highland Treasure Trilogy Box Set

Much Ado About Highlanders (Scottish Relic Trilogy Book 1)

Taming the Highlander (Book 2)

Tempest in the Highlands (Book 3)

Scottish Relic Trilogy Box Set

Love and Mayhem

The Promise (Pennington Family)

The Rebel

Secret Vows Box Set

Borrowed Dreams (Scottish Dream Trilogy Book 1)

Captured Dreams (Book 2)

Dreams of Destiny (Book 3)

Scottish Dream Trilogy Box Set

Romancing the Scot

It Happened in the Highlands

Sweet Home Highland Christmas

Sleepless in Scotland

Dearest Millie

How to Ditch a Duke

A Prince in the Pantry

Highland Crown (Royal Highlander Series Book 1)

Highland Jewel (Book 2)

Highland Sword (Book 3)

Ghost of the Thames

Thanksgiving in Connecticut

Made in Heaven

Jane Austen Cannot Marry

Erase Me

Marriage of Minds: Collaborative Writing *(Nonfiction)*

Step Write Up: Writing Exercises for 21st Century *(Nonfiction)*

* * *

NIK JAMES NOVELS

Caleb Marlowe Westerns

High Country Justice

Bullets and Silver

The Winter Road

Silver Trail Christmas

* * *

JAN COFFEY NOVELS

Trust Me Once

Twice Burned

Triple Threat

Fourth Victim

Five in a Row

Silent Waters

Cross Wired

The Janus Effect

The Puppet Master

Blind Eye

Road Kill

Mercy

When the Mirror Cracks

Tropical Kiss

Aquarian

Omid's Shadow

Erase Me

May McGoldrick

Jan Coffey

Book Duo Creative

Thank you for choosing *Erase Me*. In the event that you enjoy this book, please consider sharing the good word(s) by leaving a review, or connect with the authors.

Erase Me

Copyright © 2024 by Book Duo Creative LLC

All rights reserved. Except for use in any review, the reproduction or utilization of this work in whole or in part in any form by any electronic, mechanical or other means, now known or hereafter invented, including xerography, photocopying and recording, or in any information storage or retrieval system, is forbidden without the written permission of the publisher: Book Duo Creative LLC.

Cover by Dar Albert, WickedSmartDesigns.com

Enjoy!
Nikoo & Jim

Mary / Jim

Love is timeless...

To Judy Reed, our precious friend

Thank you for lending us Michael

Chapter One

Avalie

San Clemente, California

THE BATTERED copy of *Pride and Prejudice* that nestled on the end of the twenty-five-cent shelf caught my eye, and a jolt of excitement threaded through me. Only a chest-high metal railing, a few steps, and a half-dozen people separated me from my bargain find.

I tried to edge around an elderly couple. "Excuse me. Can I get by you?"

In front of the beach town's library and the used-book annex, the Sunday Farmers Market stretched along the sidewalks of Del Mar, the main street of San Clemente's downtown. Shoppers pushed through crowded tents and tables filled with fresh produce and honey, olive oil and cheeses. And from the look of the throng combing through the racks of books, the Friends of the Library store was doing equally well.

My eyes remained locked on the treasured book as I made my way closer. Polite requests were met with reluctant shuffling. As I edged past strollers and dog walkers, it seemed that everyone had chosen this precise moment to reconnect with long-lost acquaintances or discuss the latest happenings in the sleepy oceanside town.

Finally, my prize was only a few steps away. As my fingers extended towards the used copy of the Jane Austen classic, a man's hand reached out and took it. Disappointment prickled down my spine.

"You wanted this?" I asked. "You sure?"

"I *did* want it," he replied, pausing before holding the book out to me. "But you can have it."

Surprised, I looked up into his face, and my heart stopped. He stood a lanky six feet, and sandy-colored hair that fell over his collar framed a square-jawed face. The dark brown eyes sparkled in the June sunlight. There was a hint of amusement in them, and they seemed to invite me into a world of possibility and adventure. He was dressed in a plain blue T-shirt and jeans that did nothing to hide his muscled chest and arms. And his easy stance gave him a look of balance and confidence. But it wasn't his physical attributes that caused me to take a second look; it was the mischievous, somewhat lopsided grin.

"Are you sure?" I asked, taking the book.

"Absolutely. Everyone needs multiple copies of their favorite book."

"What makes you think I already have it?"

"Doesn't every woman who reads have a copy or two?" he asked confidently.

A shopper bumped me, causing me to nearly drop the precious find. I held it close to my chest.

"In fact, I'll bet you have your favorite pages dog-eared."

Running my fingers along the ream of the book in hand, I held it up to him as proof. "No dog ears here."

"You haven't taken it home yet."

"You have no idea what I do to things that I take home."

"Books or people?"

The lopsided grin had never left his face. Our eyes met and I recognized the spark of interest. "Let's keep the conversation about books."

"Whatever you say." He nodded. "Well, *do* you have another copy of *Pride and Prejudice*?"

"I actually do have another copy, but I didn't bring it with me on this trip."

"So you're not a local?"

"No. You?"

"Visiting San Clemente for the first time."

"Me too," I confessed.

Another shopper with a toddler strapped to her back noticed the book in my hand. "Oh my God! My book club is reading *Pride and Prejudice*. Can I have this copy?"

I gathered it tightly against my chest. "Sorry, I was here first."

"It's not technically yours until you pay for it."

The handsome stranger put a hand on my elbow and nodded toward an elderly woman collecting payments at a table a few steps away. I shoved a hand into my jacket pocket and flashed my credit card.

The young mother pointed to the sign next to the box. "Cash only."

Cash. I patted the jacket and my short pockets. I had no cash.

My rival for the book held out her hand. "I'll take that from you, thank you very much,"

She didn't know me. I wasn't one to retreat from battle. "Is there an ATM anywhere near here?"

"For God's sake, it's twenty-five cents." She bounced her

complaining child on her back. "I don't have all day. Let me have it."

"No." I clutched the book tighter in my chest.

"I've got it," the handsome stranger interrupted, holding up a ten-dollar bill.

"You don't have to do that."

He shook his head and handed the money to the cashier, telling the white-haired woman to keep the change. He tried to take the book out of my hand, but I was clutching it tight.

"I promise to return it to you."

I let go and watched him as he made a show of sliding it into a brown paper bag he'd picked up off the table. He handed it to me as mother and toddler huffed off.

"Are you two together?" the library volunteer asked, amused.

"Maybe," he said with a wink. He turned to me. "You promised to feed me, didn't you?"

Confident. Definitely confident. And charming.

We made our way through the crowd and stopped in front of a vendor's table piled high with fresh artisan bread. The scent of herbs, garlic, and sourdough wafted in the air.

"You paid too much," I told him.

"Bailing you out of jail would have cost much more."

"It wouldn't have gone that far."

"Yes, it would have. I saw the flash in your eyes. You were ready to flatten that woman."

Shrugging my shoulders, I smiled. "Okay, a dollar would have been a fair price." I held the bag out to him. "You overpaid and the book *is* technically yours."

"No. Add it to your Austen collection when you get home." He glanced at a red trolley that rang a bell as it moved down Del Mar on the other side of the line of tents. "Wherever home is."

He was fishing for information. I had my book. I could have

walked away. But I didn't, waiting to see what his next move was.

Del Mar was a pretty, tree-lined street of small shops and restaurants. The abundance of red-tile roofs and white stucco walls made it picture-perfect Southern California. El Camino Real, the original Spanish road that connected missions and small forts, crossed Del Mar at the top of the street, forming a tee. From where I was standing, the road ran down to the ocean, where a long heavy-timbered pier guarded miles of white sand beaches. In short, San Clemente was gorgeous.

"Are you hungry?" he asked.

"Starved."

"Can I buy you breakfast? Or is it lunch already?"

I glanced at the clock tower over the library and was surprised to learn how much of the day was already gone.

"Lunch is on me, so long as they accept credit cards," I told him.

A pair of women walking by smiled at him, and he smiled back. *A player*.

"You'll change your mind about paying as soon as you see how much I eat."

"Fair enough."

"Reed."

I stared at his outstretched hand. Did people shake hands these days? Didn't it go away with Covid? "Reed...?"

"That's all. My friends call me Reed."

"Avalie," I put my smaller hand in his. His fingers were calloused, his grip strong.

"Avalie...?"

"That's all you need to know...today."

He smiled. Across Del Mar from where we stood, a charming building with Spanish-inspired architecture housed an outdoor café serving food. The white stucco walls were adorned with colorful ceramic tiles, and a wrought iron sign above the entrance displayed the café's name in elegant cursive.

"What do you think?" I asked.

He put a hand on my elbow, and we crossed the street. As we approached the café, we noticed a line of people waiting to get inside.

"We can go somewhere else," Reed suggested.

"If you can wait that long, so can I."

He put our name down on the waiting list, and we drifted toward a low stone wall that offered a surface to lean against. His long legs stretched out against mine, creating an intimate connection. He leaned in a bit closer as others tried to share the same stretch of wall. A menu was passed along to those waiting. I stared at the colorful page.

"Vegan? Vegetarian, gluten-free? What do you eat, or don't eat?"

"One of everything on this menu. They all look good." I passed on the menu to the person next to me. "You're not the only person who can pack it away."

His chuckle was a warm whisper in my ear. "So, where's home?"

"San Francisco," I told him. "You?"

"New York City. What brings you here?"

"Girlfriends' reunion."

"Is that a thing?"

"Don't you have a reunion with *your* girlfriends?"

"Ha! That's a good idea. How does it work?"

"We get away once a year. A bunch of us, all good friends from college, rent a house at some destination and whoever gets there, gets there."

He shook his head. "That won't work for me."

"Which part doesn't work? Once a year? Bunch of your girlfriends?"

"Neither."

Three young women, all about the same height with the same shoulder-length bleached blond hair, all wearing shorts and bikini tops, talking loudly amongst themselves, walked past the restaurant. Reed's eyes followed them for a few seconds before turning back to me.

"What about the rest of your friends? Everyone still sleeping?"

"I'm the first one to arrive in San Clemente."

"When did you arrive?" he asked.

"Last night."

"And the rest?"

"They're coming whenever they can get away. If they can get away." I pushed the cell phone deeper into my pocket.

"Are you saying they might not show up?"

"Everyone except me has real responsibilities."

"What's a real responsibility these days?"

There were more pregnant women and multiple babies in strollers on this street than I'd ever seen on any other street in my life. "Motherhood, spouses, serious nine-to-five office jobs, I guess."

"And you don't have any of those things?"

"The rental was paid for way in advance. I have a job that I can take on the road, so I packed the laptop and voilà, I'm here. First to arrive. Sun and surf. Carefree and ready to have a good time."

"What about the rest of it?"

Tilting my head, I stared into his brown eyes.

"Motherhood, spouses, partners?"

"Not ready for those kinds of grownup commitments." I shook my head. "Enough about me. How about you? Give me the a-to-z of it."

"What happens if no one else shows up?"

"I'll be wandering in and out of bookstores, trying to not get into fights with mothers and toddlers."

"I can help you with that." He smiled, his shoulder bumping mine. "A week, I mean, keeping you out of trouble."

"Who mentioned a week? We could have booked the place for the weekend."

"It's already Sunday, and a guy could only hope."

Thirty-two years old and I'd been with enough men to recognize when someone was making a move on me. He *was* gorgeous and sexy and definitely making a move on me. The prospect was interesting.

"They've done it to me in the past. Cancelling on me, I mean. So who knows? I might end up on my own."

The sun was warm...or was it the air, or the delicious heat radiating from the man standing so close next to me? I shed my jacket and draped it over my arm.

Two parties of four were called. The waiting line of people moved. Reed put a hand on the small of my back and slid us down the line closer to the restaurant. Standing sideways, his fingers stayed on the newly exposed band of skin between my halter top and khaki shorts, caressing ever so softly. My bare shoulder pressed into his chest. He was all muscle underneath.

A jolt of awareness had run through my body the first moment I laid eyes on him. Now, it was even stronger. Whatever was happening here was totally unexpected.

The question popped in my head. *When was the last time I had sex?* It had to be way too long as I couldn't remember.

"What is it that you do?" I asked.

"You don't want to know."

"Oh, I do."

"I've got the most boring job in the world."

"No, I own that one. I've got that title after my signature."

"Maybe we do the same thing."

"I doubt it." I shook my head.

"But you haven't told me what you do." He was clever about directing the questions away from himself.

"I'm a freelance editor for technical magazines. I tell people who can't write where to put commas and exclamation marks."

"That *is* boring."

"I told you. Now you. What do you do?"

"I handle commercial property insurance."

"You go on the road for that?" I asked.

"You have to, especially when your customers are in a high-risk fire hazard zone and my company is thinking about canceling their policies."

"Ouch, that hurts. Do they know that's why you are here?"

"I assume so. Other insurance companies are doing the same thing."

"Purging their livelihood. Cutting the cord. Pulling the rug from under their dreams. The terminator."

"Put it that way, it sounds pretty harsh."

"Your job isn't boring. It's shitty."

"Okay. We're both unhappy with what we do." His eyes moved over my face. "Let's look at the perks. Like, right now. This moment. Neither of us is on the clock. Are we?"

His fingers moved to my bare back as we shifted down the line again.

"When did *you* get here?" I asked Reed.

"Last night."

"How long are you staying?"

"A week or two, maybe more. It all depends on the job."

"Who did you check in with when you landed?"

His head dipped and his face moved closer to mine. "You mean my boss?"

"No. I mean wife, girlfriend, boyfriend, husband." I didn't get the vibe from him, but I still had to ask.

"Does it make a difference?"

"Absolutely. I don't have sex with people who are in relationships."

He moved closer to me. Without warning, he reached up and ran his thumb over my bottom lip. I sucked in a breath.

"So we're going to fuck, are we?"

"Depends. You haven't answered my question."

"No one. There was no one I had to call."

"No one you had to call? Or no one who gets upset if you and I have sex."

"Yes to both. I'm not into relationships."

"Why not?"

"I move around too much."

"You don't have sex?"

"Oh, I have sex. And I'm good at it. We were talking about relationships and commitment."

There was a time in my life when a statement like that would have prompted a thousand and one more questions from me. But not anymore. Not in this situation. He already had me hooked.

"That settles it." I lifted myself on my toes and kissed him, hot enough, thoroughly enough that the front of his jeans pressing against me told me I had his attention.

"Fuck lunch," he breathed. "Let's go."

We were one group away from getting a table. "How about food?"

"I'll feed you after." He took my hand, and we pulled out of line.

"Where are we going?" I asked.

"Where are you staying?"

"Renting a house a couple of blocks over, on Avenida Victoria."

"Lead the way."

"No. Any of my girlfriends could get in today. This morning, in fact. I'm not into explaining us. Where are you staying?"

"The same street, actually."

"Your place it is, then."

Erase Me

Half a block up crowded Delmar, we took a right and into an open parking area connecting two blocks. The lot was a chaotic mix of parked cars, surfboards strapped to roof racks, and families loading their finds from the farmer's market.

"Please tell me you have nobody who will pop in unannounced," I teased, trying to match my steps to his long strides.

"No roommates, no neighbors that I've met yet. You're my first and only friend in San Clemente."

"I can't remember the last time I was first at something."

"We'll see if we can fix that right now."

I don't know which one of us first saw the man squatting next to his pile of belongings at the end of the parking lot. He was directly in our path. We both reacted and tried to go around him. But the disheveled stranger suddenly sprang to his feet, blocking our way. He wore worn, grimy clothing that clung to a thin frame. His unwashed hair hung in greasy tangles, partly obscuring his eyes, which flickered with intensity as he stared at us.

Reed's fingers tightened around my hand.

The stranger's face was etched with scars, a roadmap of past battles, and his eyes darted about, constantly surveying the surroundings nervously. From where we stood, a couple of steps away, the musty odor of the man's clothing clashed starkly with the lunchtime aroma wafting from the surrounding restaurants.

Reed pulled my hand and we tried to move around him, but the stranger continued to block our path.

"You." He pointed a gnarled and dirty finger at Reed, his voice a jarring mixture of anger and desperation. "I've seen you before."

My eyes flicked to Reed. A mixture of wariness and confusion marked his expression.

"I doubt it."

"Don't lie to me." The man bristled.

"You've got the wrong guy." Reed's tone was calm, attempting to defuse the situation.

Pulling me with him, he again attempted to sidestep the menacing figure. However, the man moved with us, blocking our path and glaring.

"You walked out of the water," he said. "Like a demon rising from the ocean, you walked right out."

An older woman was standing a few steps away, loading shopping bags into her car. "You want me to call the cops on him?"

The man showed no interest in her.

"No, that's okay. He's confused." I pulled Reed away from the stranger, and the woman got in her car.

As we made a wide arc across the lot, the man's voice followed us.

"I have your bag," he shouted. "I have it. And you know what's in there. Come and get it. You know where to find me. Come and get it."

Chapter Two

Avalie

PLANTING both palms on the edges of Reed's bathroom sink, I stared at my reflection in the mirror. My short, pixie-cut dark hair was standing up on end, giving me a look that was more porcupine than pixie. My face was flushed. The brown pupils of my eyes were dilated. My palms were still sweating. I touched a tender spot on my right breast.

"Shit. Shit. Shit." Having sex the first day in San Clemente wasn't part of the plan. There were places I needed to be, things I had to do.

Closing my eyes and taking a few deep breaths, I tried to line up my thoughts, make sense of what I had done and everything that lay ahead. Instead, I thought of Reed, lying naked in that bed.

He was hot and good at sex. No, great actually. He knew all the right buttons to push until I was putty in his hands. Not that I needed any encouragement or would have objected to anything he suggested. After all, I initiated the whole thing.

But why?

Was it his eyes? His confidence? Was it the immediate chemistry between us? The spontaneous eruption of heat that raced through me?

Maybe, but it was also something else. From the moment I arrived here, I'd been feeling the glow of a sensual *something*. My skin was tingling. I was eating more, drinking more. In some ways, my body still didn't feel put together right. Still, everything had gone a little haywire from the moment Reed reached for that copy of *Pride and Prejudice*.

Seriously, how could I resist having sex with a six-foot hunk who appreciated classic literature?

I was not about to give him any slack about his comment about women and their 'dog-eared' copies of Austen's book, but I'd often thought that I couldn't be the only person whose mind conjured up images of sex with Darcy.

Reed's apartment, nestled on the third floor, was accessible via stairs that clung to the exterior of the building. The open living area was sparsely furnished, and what was there was well-worn. An oversized TV on one wall, a sectional sofa. A table and chairs by an open kitchen door. A couple of large vases with tired-looking dried flower arrangements. Some cutesy folk art on the walls that had text on them like, 'This way to the Beach' and 'Kowabunga, Dude!' A sliding glass door led to a balcony facing the street, which was large enough for a table and a couple of chairs.

As soon as I tossed my jacket and the bag on the sofa, the tour ended. With his lips on mine, Reed lifted me in his arms like I weighed nothing and carried me to his bed.

Splashing cold water on my face now, I urged myself to do no daydreaming about what happened. If I let myself do that,

I'd probably be crawling back into bed with him for an encore performance.

Taking another look at my reflection in the mirror with an objective eye, I accepted that this was long overdue. I'd enjoyed the touch of a man who knew his way around a woman's body. True, I'd been busy with work lately, but I'd forgotten the afterglow that went with spontaneous sex.

I touched my warm face with my palms. It had been way too long. Turning on the shower, I did a quick rinse and turned off the water.

Reed had still been in bed when I slipped into the bathroom. As I pushed back the shower curtain, there was a tap on the door, and the handle moved.

I'd locked the door. I wondered if he expected to be let in.

"Are you okay in there?" he asked.

"Yeah. Be right out."

"Still hungry?"

"Starved."

"Any food preference?"

"No."

"Good, because I already ordered to have some sandwiches delivered from a lunch place around the corner," he said from the bedroom as he walked away.

Picking up a folded towel from a shelf, I dried myself and wrapped it around me.

He called from the kitchen. "Coffee's almost ready. Would you prefer something else to drink?"

"No, coffee is perfect."

"Okay, I also have..." Silence for a moment. "The food's here. They're downstairs. I'll be right back."

I cracked the door and heard him go out. Crossing through the bedroom, I slipped into the living area, where I saw the door of the apartment was ajar. I closed it.

Taking a quick look around the apartment, I spotted

another door that led into a second bathroom, smaller than the one I took a shower in. There was also a locked door that was most likely another bedroom where the owners kept their personal belongings.

I hurried back to the bedroom and stopped in the doorway.

Where an hour ago Reed and I had made use of every inch of the king-size bed, the bedspread was now neatly pulled up and the pillows arranged by the headboard.

He'd draped my clothes over the back of a chair, and my cell sat on the cushion. Dropping the towel, I quickly pulled on my shorts and halter top and tucked the phone into my back pocket.

The men I typically hooked up with were usually easy to get into bed with but even easier to dismiss afterward. Inevitably, there was some irritating trait that was quick to surface. Reed, however, seemed to be an exception. No flaws yet.

"But there's still time," I murmured.

Reed. I didn't even know the rest of his name. Scanning the room, my eyes immediately fell on a wallet on the dresser. Glancing once more toward the closed apartment door, I crossed the room and picked up the wallet. It was the folding type, brand new and surprisingly light. I opened it to find around a couple of hundred dollars in cash, one credit card, and a driver's license. No membership cards, no library ID, no pictures, no random receipts.

Didn't men normally stuff their wallets with things like that?

I pulled out the driver's license. Reed Michael. The picture had to be taken recently. The issuing state was New York, just as he'd told me.

"Are you legit, Reed Michael?"

Taking my phone out of my pocket, I quickly sent a text message, accompanied by a photo of Reed's license.

- *I need you to check this guy out for me*
- *Why?*

- I had sex with him
- What the fuck
Exactly.

I slipped the phone back into my pocket and left Reed's wallet exactly where I'd found it. I slid open the closet door. No suitcases or bags. The words of the man in the parking lot came back to me. *I have your bag. You know what's in there.*

A few shirts, pants, jeans, a pair of sweatshirts, and a cotton sweater had been hung carefully on hangers. As I ran my fingers along the crisp textures, I noticed the price tag on the first and then the second item. None of them had been worn before. Every piece of clothing still bore its original tag.

"What are you looking for?"

I almost jumped out of my skin. It wasn't like me to get caught. After waiting a couple of seconds for my heartbeat to settle into its normal rhythm, I glanced over my shoulder at Reed, who was picking up my wet towel off the floor.

"Got a sweatshirt I can borrow?"

"Sure, take anything you want. Just rip the tag off."

"Went shopping last night?"

"They lost my luggage. I had to."

"Sorry about the towel. I'll take that."

He handed it to me. "You can hang it behind the bathroom door. The food is here."

I watched him go toward the kitchen. Taking a navy blue sweatshirt from the hanger, I examined the tag and the store where he had bought it. I inspected a couple more pieces of clothing. They were all purchased from the same place. Tearing off the price tag, I pulled the sweatshirt over my head.

Stepping back into the bathroom, I took one more look at my reflection and ran a hand through my wet hair. My eyes were clear. The stubborn set of my jaw had returned. I glanced at my phone. No response from Payam yet.

Reed was in the kitchen, arranging the food on a platter when I got there.

"You locked me out." He motioned toward the door of the apartment.

"Habit. Not used to running around naked with the door open."

His eyes darkened as he gave me the once-over. "Did you find what you were looking for?"

"No. I prefer pinks and purples and colors livelier than what you got in there."

"That's good to know. I'll remember for the next time."

"The next time you go shopping?" I gave him a look. "Airlines lose your luggage a lot?"

"Considering how often I travel, yes. More than I like."

"Don't they find your bags and deliver them to you?"

"Eventually." He took two plates from a cabinet. The platter on the counter was heaped with sandwiches and fries. "Are you surprised that I can shop? I thought women love that in a man."

"Don't paint all of us with one brush. Why would you assume that?"

"First books. Now shopping. Okay, that's two things, but I'm really not one to lump all women together."

I crossed my arms over my chest. "Are we having our first fight?"

He smiled. "No way. I'm too hungry to fight."

Reed picked up the plates and silverware and the platter of food and motioned with his head toward the coffee pot.

"Would you mind pouring a couple of mugs? I take mine black."

"Can we eat outside?"

"Definitely."

As he passed me, he stopped, leaned close, and brushed his lips against mine. "Did I tell you how much fun I had this morning?"

I pressed my forehead against his. "Technically, it may have been noon. And I had fun too."

Because I didn't want him to have the last word or the last gesture, I kissed him again, deeper, teasing him, until I sensed he was thinking about me more than about food. Then I pulled back and pushed him out of the kitchen.

"Two black coffees, coming right up."

I listened to his footsteps padding across the floor. As the porch door slid open, I pulled out my cell phone. Still no return message.

I typed quickly. - *What are you doing*

- *Chasing your lover's rap sheet*

- *Send me what you got.*

- *Not ready yet*

- *WTF. You used to be good at this stuff*

- *Oh I am. And you know it. Now go and have another quickie and stop harassing me.*

- *Things are getting too cozy*

- *For you that's bad.*

- *Exactly. Oh I need one more thing.*

- *What*

- *In about 15 minutes or a half-hour call me and get me out of here*

Taking some mugs from the same cabinet where he had gotten the plates, I poured the coffee.

- *Which is it? How much time*

- *No more than 30*

"Can you grab some napkins on your way out?" Reed called out.

I stuffed the phone in my pocket, picked up the mugs, and grabbed the napkins.

Reed watched me as I came out onto the porch. The table and chairs had been arranged against the porch railing.

"I'll take that."

I put down the napkins, handed him a coffee, and stood next to him.

Houses of various shapes and sizes lined Avenida Victoria, and a blue slice of the Pacific Ocean was visible in the distance.

"Beautiful view. You must enjoy some breathtaking sunsets from here."

"I don't know. I guess I'll find out tonight."

Shifting my focus to the east, uphill, I immediately spotted the house. Positioned in the center of the block and occupying the space of three houses, the white stucco structure featured a red tile roof, arched windows, and wings extending out from both sides of the central building. Several balconies on the second floor faced Reed's place. From where we were sitting, I had a perfect view of not only the front of the house but of a number of the west-facing windows.

"I've noticed that house too. Pretty nice. And that's a lot of square footage for this street."

"Yeah," I said, trying to hide my surprise at how closely he was watching me.

"I don't think anyone is living there."

"Really? How do you know?" I asked.

"I don't. Only guessing from the way things are buttoned up."

It was true that the shades in every window were drawn shut. Outdoor furniture on the ground-floor patios had been covered with dark green tarps, blinds were closed, and awnings on the second-floor balconies had been drawn in.

"They might be on vacation."

"Maybe." Reed gestured up the street. "So you're staying up that way?"

I nodded and sipped my coffee. "I'm way up the hill."

He put an arm around me. "Walking distance."

"Are we making plans past this morning?"

"I'd like to."

He moved behind me and pressed his lips to my neck. It was easy to press my back into his chest, to have his arms close around me. I turned sideways to study his face. In the sunlight, his hair had naturally golden highlights in the sandy brown. And those dark eyelashes. They were long and the perfect accent for the brown eyes that watched me with such intensity.

My brain flashed back to the two of us in bed. I definitely enjoyed it. Maybe too much. I took hold of his wrist and moved out from his encircling arms. Going around the table, I sat down.

"What did you order for us?"

"If I ordered the right things, does that mean we'll do this again?"

I couldn't help but smile. "I hope you got it right."

"So much pressure." He scoffed and sat in the chair across from me. He pointed to each of the sandwiches. "Turkey Avo, Veggie Lovers, Best Reuben Ever."

"How do you know this is the *best* Reuben ever if you've never had it before?"

"That's what it's called on the menu."

"You trust everything you read?" I teased.

"A hundred percent. I'm the most trusting person you ever met."

Maybe, but a shadow of doubt had already entered the picture. Payam was the most accomplished and efficient assistant I'd ever had, and there was still nothing getting reported back. Not a good sign. I guessed that Reed's information was turning out to be a bit more complicated than just plugging his license number into the data files of the New York State Motor Vehicle Department. Definitely not a good sign.

"Start." He motioned to the food. "Please."

The sandwiches were huge. Thankfully, they were divided into quarters. "You must have guests coming that you haven't told me about."

"I warned you about how much I eat."

Taking a section of the Veggie Lovers sandwich, I pulled out my cell and put it on the table, next to my plate.

"Expecting a call?"

"You never know with the crew I travel with. Any one of them could be at the house right now, trying to figure out how to get in."

"And you have the only key."

"That's me. Master of the key."

"The one that can open every door."

"Actually and metaphorically."

He tapped my coffee mug with his. "I'll drink to that."

He stretched out his long legs, and the intentional brush of his bare feet against mine sent a subtle shiver through me. There was an unmistakable appeal about the way he remained acutely attuned to me.

I absorbed the warmth of the moment, but I couldn't shake the awareness that this connection couldn't last. A fling was one thing, but I wasn't home. Here it would be stupid—possibly dangerous—to form any kind of attachment to this man while on a mission. The sex would have to do. But in this fleeting instant, I couldn't help embracing the delicate and passionate dance between us.

"I meant to ask you about Austen," I asked.

"What about Austen?"

"Why were you going to buy that book?"

"Who said I was buying it?"

"You grabbed it before I did."

"I picked up a number of books before you got there and put them back."

Swallowing the bite of the sandwich, I leaned toward him. "Wait, are you embarrassed to admit that you were interested in Austen?"

"Why should I be embarrassed?"

"Have you ever read any of her books?"

"No."

"Do you know what they are?"

"Romances."

"Sort of. But do you actually read romances?"

"Are you saying men don't read romances?" He tried to look shocked. "Because that would sound a lot like a broad-brush generalization to me."

"No, I wasn't." I took a big bite of the sandwich and watched him intently as he ate.

He broke the momentary silence. "Okay, what do you want to know? Your eyes are like black lasers."

"Black lasers," I scoffed. "How romantic!"

"How's this?" He paused dramatically. "Your eyes, like the darkness of deepest midnight, bathe the depths of my soul, igniting a love that burns brighter than a thousand stars. Better?"

Laughter bubbled out of me. "And you're a poet too."

The feigned look of innocence, as he pretended he meant what he'd said, was even funnier.

"Fine, fine," he finally said, smiling. "What do you want to know?"

"*Pride and Prejudice.* Austen. *Your* generalization about all women having a dog-eared copy? Come clean. You were going to buy that book."

He reached for another portion of a sandwich. "I was curious about why is it that a copy of Austen's book would be more important to a woman than a half dozen boxes of her belongings."

I sat back in my chair and looked at him over the rim of my coffee mug. I hated to admit it, but Reed might be the most perfect man I'd ever met. I was almost sorry to ask the logical next question. "Why do I feel like I'm missing a story here."

Reed sighed. "This morning, you asked me if there was someone I had to call when I arrived here."

I leaned forward in my chair. "Shit. So you *are* married."

"No. No, I'm not," he said quickly. "And I'm not in any kind of permanent relationship, either."

"Girlfriend?"

"No. Not now. But there used to be one. There was a woman that I lived with."

"For how long?"

"Does it matter?"

"As far as context goes, yes."

"Okay. Six months. No, it was less," he corrected. "But can I get back to telling the Austen part of the story?"

I took another quarter of a sandwich. "Please do. I've been waiting all day."

His eyes sparked with a playful glint, amused that I was teasing him. "Over that very, very, *very* short time that we were together, she'd moved boxes and boxes of her stuff into my apartment. Now, the weird part? When we called it quits, after that *exceptionally* short period, I carefully boxed up all of her belongings, thinking she'd want them back. Imagine my surprise when she showed up, took just one thing, and casually suggested I donate the rest."

"The one thing. Was it Jane Austen?"

"An old, dog-eared copy of *Pride and Prejudice*." He shrugged. "That's the only thing she wanted."

I raised my coffee mug. "A woman with excellent taste. You clearly let a good one go. She and I could have been friends."

He shook his head and smiled, pushing to his feet. "You have a very strange sense of humor. Do you want more coffee?"

"Yes, please." I handed him my cup.

Just as Reed reappeared with the coffee mugs, my phone rang. Half an hour. Right on the dot. Payam was good. I rose to my feet and moved along the railing.

I started right in. "I'm already here. As always, the first one."

"Do you really expect me to carry on a conversation here?" Payam retorted.

"No, of course not." I listened to Reed settle into his chair behind me. "Our apartment is nothing to brag about, but we're walking distance to downtown and the Pier."

"You ask my location, now," Payam reminded me.

"Right. Where are you now?"

"Wasting my time on the phone with you."

I turned around, leaning against the railing, aware that Reed was attentively observing and listening to our conversation. "Do you have what we talked about?"

"I would and I will if you'd end this fucking phone call."

"Okay. Well, with no traffic, you should be at the apartment in fifteen to twenty minutes."

Blasted Payam ended the call, and I had to carry on like my roommate was still on the phone.

"Have you heard from anyone else?"

Staring at my bare feet, I tried to weave the story I intended to tell Reed.

"No worries. We'll figure it out when you get here." Pause. Smile. "I'll be waiting at the apartment. Bye."

I ended the call and pushed the phone into my back pocket.

He raised his cup of coffee. "Well, sounded like that wasn't a cancellation."

I nodded. "I have to go."

He stood up and walked toward me. "Who is this friend?"

"Pat."

"Married, kids, responsibilities?"

"Check, check, check."

He wrapped his arms around me and pulled me to his chest. His body rubbed suggestively against mine. "We don't live that far apart. Does she go to bed early?"

I was already feeling bad about the lie. The sex was good, I liked him, and I would have enjoyed nothing more than crawling back into the bed and picking up where we'd left off. But I couldn't.

I shook my head. "When Pat gets away from her family, she wants quality girl time and serious girl talk. And boy, you wouldn't believe how much and how long she can talk."

Pressing my lips against his, I intended to give him a peck on the lips, but he caught me off-guard, tightening the embrace and giving me the hottest kiss we'd shared yet. I was questioning my decision to go when he broke it off and backed away.

That's when I saw my phone in his hand.

"You picked my pocket."

Reed grinned. "For a good cause. You don't have my number."

He held the phone in front of my face, expecting it to unlock. I was too smart to rely on security as antiquated as that.

"Give me yours."

He handed me his phone, and I punched in my number and a second later, my phone buzzed with incoming.

"Happy?"

"For now."

"Today was really fun," I remarked, offering him a fleeting kiss, skillfully evading his grasp this time. "Can I give you a hand with these dishes?"

"No, I'm a domesticated male."

"Yeah, okay." I paused, actually feeling a little torn. "Well, I'll see ya."

Retreating into the living room, I began to peel off his sweatshirt when Reed called from the doorway to the porch.

"Hold onto it," he instructed. "You saw my closet. There are plenty where that one came from."

"Thank you," I replied, grabbing my coat on the way out. I

could feel his eyes on me, tracking my movements until I closed the door behind me. Descending the stairs to the street, I reminded myself that it was the right decision. Despite Reed's looks, the sex, and the interesting conversation, I hadn't come to San Clemente for a relationship.

This one time together was it.

Out on the street, I cast a glance up toward his balcony, but there was no sign of him. From this vantage point, I couldn't see into the apartment. Instead of going up the hill to the dingy place I was renting, I directed my steps down the street toward the water. Since arriving in San Clemente, I had yet to put my feet in the sand or feel the clean, cold waters of the Pacific Ocean around my ankles.

A block away from Reed's apartment, my phone buzzed with a text from Payam.

- *You got anything on him?*
- *Oh, I got a lot on him*

I stopped at a corner.

- *Spill it*
- *The license is fake. Facial recognition was a no-go*
- *Come on. So who is he*
- *Let me put it this way, you slept with the enemy*

Chapter Three

Reed

I PUT the mugs and platter of food on the kitchen counter and stared at the red-tiled roof of the house next door. What the hell was I doing? And why wasn't this bothering me?

Picking up local women while I was working wasn't the norm for me. In fact, it was almost never. I took pride in my professionalism. It was a family trait. And frankly, women were a distraction I couldn't afford. The stakes were too high.

Avalie, however, was unlike most other women I seemed to run into. *Any* other woman, if I was being honest.

When we reached for the same book, I couldn't help but let my gaze linger. Her face and her body would have been enough for most men. I'm not most men, though. I can appreciate beauty without being pulled into a potentially damaging situation.

But the instant our eyes locked, something in me tightened and warmed at the same time. And I know that she felt it too.

Erase Me

Seriously, that didn't often happen—not here or at home or wherever my job took me. But this morning, aware as I was of the gut-level jolt of attraction, I had no interest in resisting it.

The provocative show of skin beneath the top she was wearing under her jacket proved to be soft and warm to my touch, and those strong, slender legs made me wish, almost immediately, for the feel of them wrapped around me.

But it was more than that. She had a surface charm to go with a wry sense of humor. She was comfortable with herself, quick, and naturally combative. My kind of woman—smart, confident and entirely fuckable.

And once she responded, my brain and body were aligned in wanting her.

No one beat my record. My commitment to the work was unchallenged. I was the best operative in our division. I had to be, given my situation. But Avalie presented something new for me, something I hadn't encountered before. It wasn't just the physical allure; there was an undeniable energy surrounding her that threatened to blur the line I'd drawn between professional commitment and personal desire. The feel was almost magnetic.

Standing at the sink, I couldn't help but acknowledge the surprising struggle between my duty and this unexpected temptation.

Running a hand down my face, I attempted to erase the lingering memories of the sex. It was better than great. Our bodies, our souls, seemed to be so connected, like two dancers so in tune with the other that they barely needed music.

Jeez, I really was starting to sound like a poet.

The interrupting call from her friend and the abrupt end to our lunch proved to be a fortunate diversion. The reason I had arrived so early in San Clemente was that I had two assignments to complete here. One was for tonight in Dana Point. The marina there was only a few miles up the shore road, but there were a few preparations I needed to complete before heading over there.

After tonight, though, I had four days free.

I went back out onto the porch and stood by the railing. Below me, a few people were going down to the pier area and the beach. Nice way to spend a Sunday afternoon. Shirtless kids and teens on electric bikes zoomed by in both directions, surfboards strapped to the sides of the bikes.

I leaned out and looked up the street. No sign of Avalie. She'd mentioned renting an apartment somewhere up there with her friends, and I couldn't help but wonder how far it was.

I double-checked the text exchange. At least, she hadn't vanished into thin air. No, I had the means to track her down.

A couple of bees seemed to be enjoying the crumbs and scraps of food left on the plates. With a gentle push, I shooed them away, picked up the remaining dishes, and went back inside. It was then that the book caught my eye. Avalie's copy of *Pride and Prejudice* sat on my sofa, where she'd dropped her jacket when we came in.

In her rush to leave, she'd overlooked the book, and I couldn't help but smile. Now I had the perfect reason to call her tomorrow.

Piling the dishes in the sink, I went back for the book. As I reached for it, my gaze caught a glint from something on the rug between the couch and the coffee table. A small cylindrical object.

Lipstick, I guessed, picturing it dropping out of Avalie's pocket.

Taking it in my hand, the lightweight metal tube measured about two inches in length and half an inch in diameter. It bore no discernible markings or seams. Giving it a closer inspection, I noticed that the inside of the tube was blocked at both ends.

"Shit."

In an instant, the realization struck me. I knew exactly what I was holding.

A weapon.

I'd seen it before. Small as it was, the device was powerful enough to stun a good-sized man. And you couldn't get one of these here. No weapon manufacturer could even produce a device like this for at least another five decades.

"What the fuck, Avalie? How the hell did you get this?"

Chapter Four

Avalie

Damn it. For the tenth time, I searched the pockets of my jacket.

Nothing. And there was no hole for the immobilizer to fall through. It had to slip out somewhere. Hopefully, not in Reed's apartment.

It might have happened there. I left in a hurry, and that small tube could have easily slid out of my pocket when I casually tossed my coat onto his sofa. I should have double-checked the pocket before leaving.

Careless. Damn it.

Maybe Reed found the weapon, but maybe he didn't. Still, given what I've learned about him since leaving his apartment, I had no doubt he would recognize the significance of the item now in his possession.

Even so, discovering who I am would be an entirely different challenge. Good luck to him with that!

Erase Me

I stood in front of the plate-glass window of my apartment and pulled my knit cap down over my ears. My earphones were secure beneath the soft wool. I zipped up my jacket. The sleek fabric conformed to the contours of my body. The familiar reflection staring back at me from the glass revealed a woman dressed head to toe in black, a warrior prepared for whatever challenges lay ahead.

Sliding my phone into my pocket, I locked the apartment door and headed down the stairs.

The street was silent and empty at this late hour. Under the dim glow of streetlamps, I navigated through a gap between some parked cars and crossed the street, moving quickly down the block. As I approached my destination, my earpieces clicked on, as expected.

"Details: security alarm, 24/7 offsite monitoring. Motion detector lights. Cameras everywhere—garage and windows. Patios and porches on all floors are equipped and monitored too. Also, besides the security company, there's an audio and visual feed, accessible remotely by the owner."

Colorado was an hour later than San Clemente. What were the odds that the owners were watching the feed live at this time of night? Still, I couldn't afford to take any chances.

"Shut everything down and run a video loop."

"They've got a hardwired backup system."

"You're a genius, Payam. Solve it."

"How much time do I have?"

"You have more eyes on the street than I do. I'm three houses from my destination. Figure it out."

"You're so fucking demanding."

I spotted the headlights of a vehicle far down the street. To be safe, I moved into the shadows of an apartment building I was passing.

No sooner had I done so when an electric bike glided silently down the street. Its rider wore dark clothing and had no running lights on the bike. From the soft voice, I realized as she approached that it was a woman; she was talking to someone on a phone. The brim of a cap kept most of her face in shadow.

She stopped at the curb two properties down from me, in front of another one of the small white Spanish-style houses that dotted the town. The headlights coming up the street belonged to a black SUV and stopped alongside her. The back window of the SUV rolled down. From where I waited, I couldn't hear much more than snippets of the conversation. Nor could I determine the number of occupants in the vehicle. But the cyclist clearly knew them.

The bicyclist's head swung toward the house where I was going. I tapped my earpiece.

"Come on, Payam. I have to go in."

"What are you dawdling for?" the voice in my ear replied. "I've been ready for you for hours."

The streetlights flickered overhead, and half a dozen of them plunged into darkness.

"Show off."

Having mapped out my route beforehand, I knew I had to cut through some backyards before reaching the door Payam had targeted for me.

"Keep an eye on the street."

"That'll be tough, won't it, since you asked me to shut things down?"

"I don't need a wise-ass remark for everything I say."

"Come on. That's why you love me."

Staying in the shadows, I cut around the next house and ran down a short driveway. I hoisted myself up onto a wooden fence and surveyed the small backyard. A row of hedges, a couple of large fruit trees, a few dark shapes that looked like lawn furniture, and another fence formed the barricade to the next yard.

As I leaped over, a dog inside barked, and a motion sensor light flickered to life as I stepped beneath it. Solar-powered lights. Ignoring them, I dashed across the yard to the next fence and jumped it in moments. The second yard remained dark, presenting an obstacle course of children's outdoor toys and a swing set. Staying close to the back wall of the house, I maneuvered to the next boundary, a six-foot concrete wall. Scaling it was no problem, but I skidded when my feet hit a lawn that was wet from water sprinklers. Somehow, I managed to stay on my feet and raced to the next fence. The dog from two houses back continued to bark.

Minutes later, after circling around a swimming pool, I climbed over one more fence and descended into the yard of my destination.

Darkness covered the backyard. From my research, I knew that the carefully landscaped gardens offered greenery and color from the terrace that extended across the back of the house. The outlines of tables and chairs were visible beneath protective coverings.

Remembering the car on the street, I wasn't about to linger here. I moved up toward the raised patio, confident that Payam was managing the security system.

As I ran toward the lower end of the house, a solar motion sensor light suddenly illuminated the patio. A few seconds later, I went through a gate onto the paved driveway. No lights here, but it wasn't difficult to find the entry door beside a three-car garage.

"Code?" I asked softly.

Payam recited the string of numbers, and with a soft click, a green light illuminated the keypad.

"Two of your friends are approaching the house. They clearly plan to enter through the patio door."

"How many...total?" I asked.

"A third one is by the shrubs in front."

"The driver? The bike rider?"

"The SUV is circling the block. The electric bike has positioned itself at the next intersection, keeping watch."

"Keep me posted if anything changes."

I was pressed for time. It was pitch-black, but I used my phone light to find the interior door. As I crossed the garage floor, I swept the light around the space. The only vehicle in here was a four-seater golf cart. A pair of surfboards and two more paddleboards hung in racks along one wall beside a workbench and a cabinet. None of this would appeal to the thugs breaking into the house.

The inside door had another security pad. "Another code?"

"Same as the last one," Payam said.

Entering the code, I went through the steel door into a short hallway. Stairs led up from the garage level to the main floor.

I was nearly at the top when I heard glass break in the front of the house. The bastards moved fast.

I knew they'd be hitting the second-floor study and bedroom, prompting me to quickly navigate through the house and position myself in the central foyer, near the foot of the stairway.

Within moments, the two intruders emerged from a front room, clad in dark coveralls with hoodies. The beams from their headlamps lit their path, and tools hung from their belts while black trash bags dangled from their hips.

They were both taller than me and, even in the coveralls, looked heavier by a large margin. Well, the bigger they are…

"What the fuck are you doing here?" I demanded, shielding my eyes.

They took a step back. I knew these people had a specific way of operating. They used a bike rider to surveil wealthy neighborhoods, looking for times when the residents were not at home. They steered clear of confrontations like the plague, never resorting to opening exterior doors or windows. They simply broke a slider or French door, and went for jewelry, cash, gold coins, or whatever they could steal. They'd be in and out of the house in fifteen minutes, where a van or SUV was waiting.

"Turn around and go out the way you came."

I didn't see the blow coming until it landed. The third intruder came out of nowhere, delivering a solid body blow to the ribs and driving me hard into a built-in bookcase at the base of the stairs. I felt the air rush out of my lungs, leaving me momentarily breathless.

The thug tried to pin me to the wall, but I wasn't about to let that happen. Striking his forehead hard with the heel of my right hand, I followed quickly with a sharp chop to his throat. He fell back, clutching his neck. In the light coming from the headlamps of his accomplices, I could see his eyes bulging as he sank to his knees.

I was sure the other two had been ready to run, but that all changed when they saw their partner go down. They were not about to leave him.

One charged at me fast, raising a hammer as he approached. One good thing about those headlamps. I knew exactly where he was looking, and the intruder's weapon of choice was clearly aimed at doing damage to my skull.

He was bigger than me but not faster. When he was two steps away, I dropped down, spun, and swept his knee. The crack told me he was going to be in a lot of pain for a while, and the hammer clattered to the floor behind me.

The last man was not as enthusiastic, but he wasn't about to leave his partners, either.

He lunged at me, screwdriver in hand. When I took hold of his wrist, he slugged me with his other fist in the ribs where I'd taken the earlier blow. Pain shot up through my body, lighting up my brain. I couldn't breathe, and I knew I had to finish this quickly.

Never letting go of his wrist, I raised my knee and slammed

his arm down on it. That was all it took. The screwdriver dropped harmlessly.

He cried out and dropped to one knee, holding his arm. Whatever fight he had in him immediately disappeared. A broken arm can do that.

I grabbed him by the collar, yanked his headlamp off, and hauled him to his feet.

The intruder who had caught me off guard was struggling to his feet, still sucking air with difficulty. The hammer-wielding thug was curled up on the floor, clutching his knee and moaning loudly.

"You two, take this one and go." My voice was strained, but I managed to bark the words out.

They'd all had enough. The two injured men somehow helped the whimpering hammer man to his feet. Leaning on each other for support, the trio staggered toward the door.

I took the lead, unlatched the door, and forcefully yanked it open, never taking my eyes off of them.

The black SUV pulled up at the curb, and they all tumbled in. As the vehicle pulled away, I closed the door, leaned my back against it, and gingerly touched my ribs.

My earpiece crackled to life. "The SUV is making good time out of the neighborhood. Appears to be heading toward the highway entrance. They picked up the bike and rider too."

"Nice of you to let me know about the third man," I retorted.

"Don't blame me. I told you he was there."

I managed to catch a breath. Not a deep one, but a breath, nonetheless.

"Clean up time."

"Well done. No corpses to dispose of."

"That was touch and go for a minute there. It could have been me."

"You *poor* thing!" Payam was an artist when it came to

sarcasm. "Well, a cleaning crew is already booked by the owners for the day before their arrival on Wednesday."

I stepped into the room where the intruders had entered and aimed one of the abandoned headlamps toward the French door leading to the patio. Shards of glass littered the floor.

"Schedule the window repairs for the same time the cleaners are here."

"Got it."

I returned to the foyer, each movement sending a sharp jolt of pain through my ribs. The ache intensified as I gingerly bent down to retrieve the hammer and screwdriver from the floor.

"And make it look like an accident. A baseball or soccer ball."

"I'll take care of it."

Looking around me, I picked up a half dozen books that had been knocked to the floor when I was driven into the bookcase. I started lining them up on the shelf.

"Do you want the Sheriff's Department to grab them?"

"Not tonight. Give it a few days. But put it in your schedule for next week to call in an anonymous tip. Descriptions, license plate, and rest of it."

"Are we going to be around that long?"

I noticed a frame on a shelf above that had fallen backward. I stood it back up and looked at the family in the photograph. A handsome couple. He had his arm around her, and she was holding an infant in her arms.

"I guess that all depends on how successful I am with this next job."

Chapter Five

Reed

THE TEXT from my handler directed me to a half-empty parking lot by the harbor in Dana Point. As I drove in, I could see a marina comprised of rows of long docks and slips crowded with boats of every size and type.

Because it was late, the parking lot was not even half full, and most cars were clustered around a drop-off rotary close to a series of restaurants lining the marina. Through my open window, I heard laughter and music coming from them.

After circling the parking lot, I identified my contact. A red, 1964 Shelby Cobra convertible occupied a space six slots away from the last car. The driver waved a cellphone light at me.

Pulling up with my driver's side facing his, I watched him struggle to extract his lanky frame from behind the wheel. His short brown hair, clean-shaven face, and the sharp lines of his cheek and jaw matched the description I had received earlier.

Still, I lifted my phone's camera toward him, and the identity match was confirmed.

"Yeah, it's me. No way they're sending a lackey to deal with the boss," he quipped, leaning against his sports car.

I stepped out and sized him up. Standing at six feet tall myself, he had a height advantage of four or five inches on me. He was well-built and too large for his car.

I cast a look around the parking lot. No foot traffic. But we were parked right under an overhead street light.

"I'm Vaughn."

"Reed." I gestured towards his highly conspicuous car. "Couldn't you opt for something less noticeable?"

He turned and ran a hand appreciatively over the body. "Don't you love it? A Shell Valley replica, Pro Dart, V8 Ford Engine, 225 CFM. A fearsome beast."

"And you get me a Honda?"

"I live here. Need to maintain certain appearances. You're here today, gone tomorrow. Besides, drawing attention is the last thing you want. Am I right?"

"So you parked under this spotlight?"

"No worries. Your people called my people, and we prepped for tonight. Every security camera, here and in the entire marina, is down. No one has eyes on us."

He raised a hand before I could point out the holes in that logic.

"And no cops are coming, either. Trust me. I'm the best. I know how to work the system. That's why your department always comes to me."

"If you say so."

"One thing you should know about me, boss, I never make mistakes. I take ownership. One hundred percent. You cowboys cruise in and get the credit, but this..." He waved his hand vaguely at the town on the bluffs behind him. "This is all mine."

"Okay."

Admittedly, I was a bit of a control freak. That was a well-known fact among everyone working for me and my handlers both in and out of the division. As I glanced across the parking lot once again, I reminded myself that in over a decade of doing this job, my support personnel had never let me down. Yet.

Vaughn reached into his car and came up with a manila folder that he waved in my direction. "And before you say how antiquated this looks, there'll be no paper trail. This is for you to look at but not to take."

He opened the folder on the hood of my Honda. A dozen photos were included in a pile of documents spilling out as he separated them side by side.

He pointed at the photographs. "This is your man. Del Volpe."

I turned on the flashlight on my phone and studied the images. White with slicked back graying hair.

Vaughn shrugged. "The guy spends most of his time either screwing young women or screwing old investors. He's making a bundle in stocks and securities. Volpe knows the future."

Slender but muscular. Clearly, a man who spent *some* time in the gym. In most images, he was in a bathing suit or shorts lounging in a bar or aboard a very large yacht. Seemed to favor loud flowery shirts. In a few, he was dressed in a business suit.

"There are whispers coming out of the SEC, but nobody knows how to pin it on him. And with his track record, he'll continue to gull future investors."

Future investors. This was the heart of the matter. Someone who time-traveled from the future could use their skills and knowledge to reap tremendous profits for themselves at the expense of others...and damage history in the process.

"What he's done up to now?"

Vaughn pulled up the documents from beneath the photos and slid the first paper-clipped bundle toward me. "Timing manipulation, mostly. He's been strategically timing his buying and selling to capitalize on future market trends."

"What else?"

Vaughn pushed the second pile over.

"Insider trading. Because he knows future market movements and non-public information, he manages to pull in dupes who think they're brilliant. Greed makes fools out of people. He uses them to insulate himself and sets them up to take the fall. And that's not all." Vaughn pushed the next bundle of pages toward me. "Lately, he's been creating fake investment opportunities and luring investors into ventures that are destined to fail. It's fraud, and he doesn't mind ruining people. He caused a suicide less than a month ago. Del Volpe's a shark."

"And he's getting rich."

"Oh, yeah. Accounts offshore. Gold bullion in secure vaults from Switzerland to Singapore. He's got a beach house in Malibu, and he just bought a second home on Billionaires' Row in New York City last month."

Vaughn dropped the last pile in front of me.

"Even in the present, he's altering events by manipulating situations to ensure positive outcomes for his investments."

One thing Vaughn didn't have to tell me was that the ripples of Del Volpe's recent actions were already being felt decades into the future.

I looked in the direction of the marina. "Where is he?"

He gave me the directions to the location where the Volpe's yacht was docked.

"It's one of the smaller super yachts in the marina."

"Staff?"

"At sea, it carries nine crew members—including the captain and a chef—and Volpe has bodyguards, as well. I talked to one of the crew when he was leaving earlier. They were all going up to Newport Beach to party at a place owned by the captain.

Currently, only the chef, a steward, and the bodyguards remain onboard."

"How many?"

"Two armed goons who always shadow him. I saw them on deck just an hour ago. Also, he has company tonight. Volpe has a sweet tooth for underage women. Three girls playing dress-up were ushered down that way around dinner time. From the looks of them, I'd say there's a strong chance they'll be missing first period tomorrow at the junior high school."

Vaughn made a face in the direction of the marina. "And I mean that literally. I wouldn't put it past this guy to drop them off somewhere south of the border on his way to Cabo. Rumor is, he's done it before."

Vaughn gathered the pictures and files and put them back in the folder.

"That's it?"

He nodded and I tossed my keys to him.

This was his side of the operation. If I failed to return from the job, Vaughn would meticulously erase from the scene any trace of my presence here on this particular date. It had to be that way. It went with the territory. If I failed, I was never here.

"I'll be close if you need help, boss."

"I won't."

As I crossed the parking lot, I couldn't help but notice the fog rolling in. They called it the 'marine layer' here in Southern California. The tourism board must have thought it sounded better. Whatever. Right now the fog was starting to cover the entire waterfront with an eerie, mysterious haze. The taste of salt lingered in the breeze drifting in over the seawalls.

I descended a broad, lighted walkway consisting of concrete steps and a median filled with palm trees and green leafy plants. Before I reached the bottom, the music coming from one of the marina restaurant bars stopped abruptly. Closing time. A laughing, inebriated couple staggering up the stairs paid no attention to me as they passed.

At the bottom of the stairs, there were tables and chairs that I'm sure were filled during the day, but they were empty now. Only a handful of people strolled along the walkways, their attention focused on their partners or the boats in the docks and slips. I wandered across to the railing, surveying the marina. It was so quiet now that I could hear the distant sounds of surf and the gentle lapping of water against the concrete wall beneath me.

Turning to the right, I moved casually toward the berth where my target's vessel was docked. The Dana Point Marina was an impressive display of expensive boats. Even though the summer season was getting into high gear, the hour was late and the majority of them sat silent and snug in their slips. Cabin lights were only visible in a few docked vessels, and they were widely scattered.

Locked security gates separated the public walking paths from the private docks. As I approached the second gate leading down to the dock, I already knew which yacht was Volpe's. It was huge and so brightly lit, the thing was probably visible from space. I could see people moving on deck.

I held my phone against the gate sensor, and the lock instantly clicked open. My handler was proving to be a pro.

Volpe's yacht was far too long to fit in any of the slips. It was anchored at the very end of the dock. Although the rest of the boats moored included luxury sailboats, yachts, and sports cruisers, they were all dwarfed by the vessel at the end.

I strolled down the dock like I owned the place. The sound of water slapping against the hulls provided a rhythmic backdrop to the laughter coming from some very young women on the deck of the boat. Vaughn was right about that. From this vantage point, I could see the bodyguards that he'd warned me about. Despite being forty yards away, they already had their eyes glued to my every move. I pretended to ignore them.

I stopped at a Sea Ray 400 Sundancer, two slips from the end of the dock, and turned down the narrow walk between boats. This boat was as good as any. The deck area in the stern was open, so I stepped onto the wide swim platform and went aboard.

The deck had bench seating and a fold-down table. Beneath one of the benches was a space with two coolers. Forward of this area was a compact galley and salon with a table for dining, and an L-shaped couch. The sliding door was unlocked. I went through and tried the door to the left of the helm. I knew it led down to the forward cabins, but it was locked.

Since I clearly owned this beauty, I must be living the good life.

I went back out to the stern deck and opened one of the coolers. A dozen beers. Perfect. They weren't cold, but it didn't matter. I didn't plan on drinking it. I pulled one out and sat on a cushioned bench where I could see the stern section of Volpe's yacht. Voices drifted toward me.

"I told you," a young woman complained loudly. "We can't stay all night."

A persuasive male voice droned some objection.

"Nuh-uh. My mother will fucking kill me," another girlish voice chimed in. "I'm late getting home already."

Definitely underage.

"*You* stay, then." He was talking to one of the girls, and his voice carried an air of confident authority. "You and I can party."

"No way, man." She had a laugh in her voice, but I could hear the nervousness beneath her tone. She was not about to be left alone with this guy.

"But we'll be back," the first girl chirped. "We can all party together. Promise."

"When?"

"Tuesday?"

"Yeah, Tuesday," the other two said in unison.

"This wolf won't be around on Tuesday," I muttered to myself.

Just then, one of the bodyguards must have decided that I was a little too close and needed checking on. As he dropped onto the dock, I popped open the beer and waited. In less than a minute, I heard his heavy tread on the walkway next to the boat.

I nodded to him as he came into view. He was squarely built with an ugly face and an even uglier haircut. When he came off the yacht, I'd seen the bulge in his windbreaker in the small of his back. He had a pistol. I had a beer. Seemed fair.

"Hey," he said. Civil, but not too friendly.

I half-turned on the bench and stretched my arm along the cushioned stern rail. "Hey back."

"Yours?" His eyes swept into the galley and dining space. Making sure there was no one else here.

"I wouldn't be sitting here if it wasn't."

"Haven't seen you around."

"Haven't *been* around."

He looked me over and then decided I wasn't worth worrying about. "This baby is sweet. How big is it inside?"

"Two cabins, a master stateroom, and a head." I looked at him coolly. "Wanna buy it?"

His eyes narrowed, unsure if I was kidding him or not. But he didn't like it. I was certainly not making a friend.

"I'll give you a good deal. Four hundred K and it's yours right now."

He stared, but I turned my head at the sound of voices. The three girls were helping each other onto the dock from the yacht. Quite the display of high heels and short dresses.

Giggling as they hung on to each other, they appeared to be drunk or high.

The bodyguard glanced at them and then back at me as his partner on the yacht called for him.

I motioned with my bottle towards the yacht. "Don't look now, but I think duty calls."

Without another word, he turned and disappeared along the walkway.

After Volpe's dates cleared out, I had a little time to kill. Occasionally, I heard low voices from the yacht. One sounded like it belonged to a woman.

Vaughn never mentioned that. Maybe he wasn't so perfect.

A few minutes later, that conversation stopped altogether. I put my feet up on the bench and listened to the muffled sound of the surf. As I waited, a single motor launch idled past on the far side, and I heard strains of some Frank Sinatra song float across the marina from a few docks over. Other than that, it was dead quiet.

Just as I decided it was time to go, I spotted my new friend coming off the yacht. A moment later, he reappeared beside my boat.

This goon and his partner must have felt I was still too close for comfort. Well, their instincts were good, at least.

"Decided to take me up on the offer?" I got up and stretched. "Normally, I'd take a check for the four hundred K, but this late at night, I only take gold bullion."

"Funny. But I actually might be interested." Very casual. Like a very burly fox. "I'd like to see the rest of the boat."

I'm sure he thought he was being clever. He knew that if this really was my boat, I'd have access to the forward cabins.

"You're serious?"

"As a heart attack at sea, pal."

I shrugged. "Okay, come aboard. Hope you don't mind the mess."

Erase Me

He stepped onto the stern swimming platform and followed me into the galley area. Here, we were out of sight of his partner on the yacht, if he was watching. And I was pretty sure he would be.

"Oh, wait. My keys," I gestured toward the bench where I'd been sitting.

That was all it took. As he turned his head, I hammered him hard on the temple with the base of my beer bottle. He went down like a sack of billiard balls. The only sound as he hit the deck was the crack of his head when it bounced.

I checked his pulse. He was out, but I didn't know for how long. I took the pistol from his waist holster.

Going out, I dropped the gun over the side and hurried along the dock to Volpe's boat. Sure enough, the other goon was staring at me from the deck.

I tried to sound scared. "Hey, a guy just slipped on my boat. I called 911, but it'll be a few minutes, they said. Can you help me? He banged his head hard."

The bodyguard stared at me for a few seconds, then hopped down onto the dock. I bolted ahead; his footsteps close behind.

When we reached the boat, he saw his partner on the deck in the dining area and shoved by me. That worked just fine.

As he crouched down, I chopped at his neck. Normally, that would have been enough to stop a bull, but this guy was only staggered a moment. He started to rise and reach for his gun at the same time.

I beat him to it, yanking the pistol from its holster and tossing it behind me. I heard it clatter across the deck outside, but I already had more pressing concerns.

The goon began to turn, but I stayed behind him, snaking my arm around his neck and clamping down hard on his windpipe.

The owner of the boat was certainly going to wonder what had happened to security in this marina, because the bodyguard threw himself backward, slamming me against the glass slider. The barrier gave way, and we toppled onto the rear deck.

He tried rolling and kicking and reaching for me. But I managed to keep clear of his big paws, and I kept squeezing. It wasn't long before I felt him start to weaken. Even a bull needs air.

I held on until he went limp...and then a little longer.

Shoving him off of me, I made sure he was still alive. He was, but just barely.

Still, I'd have to move. I didn't want these two coming up behind me.

I found the pistol on the stern deck and dropped it into the marina waters with the other.

A moment later, I was on the yacht. The boat had to be over a hundred fifty feet long, and it was plush. The stern deck was laid out for partying with large, comfortable-looking chairs and couches, a table for casual dining, and a small bar. Two sets of stairs led to the main deck where I could see wood paneling, a large salon, bar, and formal dining area.

Staying on this level, I kept moving forward, past a spotless galley and a narrow companionway that led below decks. Crew's quarters and engine room, I guessed.

Still no sign of Volpe.

Just after I passed a fully equipped movie viewing room, I heard someone coming down some steps from the main deck.

I ducked into a darkened room that turned out to be an exercise room with a pair of treadmills and racks of free weights. There was even a spa area with a sauna. This boat had everything.

A man went by with a tray tucked under his arm, humming a tune as he passed. The steward. I glanced out from my hiding place. From the back, the guy looked like a weightlifter. He turned into the galley and I heard him going down the companionway steps.

I went forward and found the steps. At the top, a passageway led past a half-dozen cabin doors, and I heard two voices coming from an open door at the very end.

Del Volpe's displeasure and frustration were evident from his tone. A woman, her voice calm and conciliatory, was attempting to placate him. As I approached, snippets of their conversation became more distinct. Listening closely, I gathered that her role involved persuading young women to join him. Tonight, however, she had fallen short. Too bad.

I glanced into the stateroom. The place was larger than the apartment where I was staying in San Clemente. And considerably nicer.

It had a sitting arrangement on the far side of a king-sized bed, by a large window of thick, one-way glass. An open walkway led to what I assumed was a bathroom. A massage table was visible there. Volpe was leading a very tough life. Practically monk-like.

On this side of the stateroom, a substantial portion of the ship's outside wall was open. Their voices were coming from there. Stepping into the room, I discovered that a retractable section of the floor extended over the water, creating an open-air balcony. It was spacious enough for four chairs arranged around a low table.

I edged into the room until I had a view of Volpe sitting in one of the chairs. The woman sat beside him. They had their backs to me and were unaware that I was behind them. On the table, I spied a plate of crackers and a block of cheese, along with an open bottle of wine chilling in an ice bucket.

"I've got to give you credit, Volpe," I said quietly. "This is the fanciest crib I've seen yet for a rogue quantum commuter."

The two were on their feet in an instant, shock registering on their faces. Her wine glass dropped out of her hand and fell into the water. He held on to his.

Confusion and fear were written all over her face. From his

expression, I knew he'd already figured out who sent me and my purpose for being here.

"But before the two of us get down to business..." I looked directly at the woman. "You need to go."

She had short, dark hair and wore jeans and a baggy navy blue sweater over a white blouse. She was quick to shake off her look of fear. As she gathered her wits, her tanned face morphed into a practiced look of disdain.

"How the fuck did you get in here?" she snapped in a British accent.

Her hands went to her pockets in an apparent search for her cell phone, but her gaze immediately went to where it sat on a table near me. I picked it up and tossed it across the room.

"Our security staff will arrive at any moment, and I assure you the police are already..."

She chattered away, but my focus remained on the object of my mission.

Volpe eyed me coolly, assessing the situation. He was taller than me by a couple of inches, and the pictures didn't lie. He had the lean, muscular look of a former athlete who had managed to keep himself in excellent condition.

"Do you want to settle our business in front of her?" I asked.

He shook his head.

"Go," he told her bluntly. "Get a room at the hotel and call me in the morning. Don't contact anyone else. I know what this is, and it doesn't involve you."

I wasn't here to mete out justice, yet I would have very much liked to see her face the consequences for providing underage girls to Volpe. As far as I was concerned, she should have spent the rest of her life in a cell, like Ghislaine Maxwell, who had performed a similar role for Jeffrey Epstein. However, Volpe had another fate in store.

With one last look at her employer, she rushed past me and disappeared through the door.

I wasn't about to waste words with this scum. "You broke the contract, and you know who sent me. So you know what we need to do."

As a time traveler, once you abandoned your mission and went rogue for personal gain, you were in a world of shit. This creep's list of crimes was a mile long. He had two options at this point. He traveled back to his original time and faced prosecution, or I finished him right here. Right now.

Either outcome worked, as far as I was concerned.

"Okay, I broke the contract. So what?" he barked. "I've been in your position. I did the job you're doing. Led that same miserable life. But I knew I deserved better. So when my chance came, I took it. I made my choice and stayed."

"Thinking you'd get away with it."

"I did...until now, didn't I?" A confident smirk pulled at his lips. "But if there's one thing I've learned, there's power in money and everyone has their price. So, what's yours? Name it."

I shook my head.

"Whatever you want, I can make it happen for you," he continued. "I have the money. What do you want? A house on the beach? Women? Name it."

Quite the salesman.

"There must be something."

His eyes darted toward the stateroom door behind me just as I heard the footsteps.

The steward I'd seen earlier came at me swinging a collapsible metal baton that would have left quite a mark if he'd been able to land it. Fortunately, his ample muscles were trained for power rather than for speed.

I caught him by the wrist and, using his momentum, slung him headfirst into the wall. The crack of his forehead against the hard paneling was definitive. Tomorrow, when he woke up, I was sure he'd be sorry he didn't take a restaurant job in some safe, quiet town far from any boats.

Before he even hit the floor, though, I expected Volpe to attack.

As I spun around to face him, I saw the wine bottle arcing toward my head. He was holding it by the neck, using it as a club. The blow glanced off the left side of my face, staggering me.

Volpe was not one to let an advantage go by. He kept coming for me, and there was murder in his eyes.

The next swing was again aimed at my head, but I stepped forward, ducking inside the trajectory of the weapon. Driving forward with my shoulder, I lifted him and felt the bottle smash against my lower back.

Together, we hit the wall beside the opening to the balcony, and the air audibly rushed from his lungs. He wasn't done, though. Jamming my face backward with his free hand, he tried to knee me in the gonads, but hit me in the thigh instead.

This guy was really beginning to wear on my goodwill.

In the periphery of my vision, I caught sight of the bottle again in the air, and he was poised to crown me with it. Not caring to wait for the possible outcome of that, I headbutted him hard, stunning him momentarily. I followed with a fierce punch to his solar plexus that robbed him of the ability to breathe.

He dropped the bottle. "Okay," he gasped. "Okay."

Showing me he was finished, he held out a hand in surrender while the other gripped his midsection.

I stood back and watched him try to draw air.

He turned toward the open balcony and took a couple of wobbling steps. He leaned on the table, and I saw the blade of the cheese knife gleaming in the light just as he snatched it up.

When he spun around to stab me, I jumped and kicked him

solidly in the chest. Volpe went crashing through the table and over the side. I went in the water after him.

I thought he had to be done, but I was wrong.

When I surfaced, the sonovabitch was lunging toward me, the knife still clutched in his hand. It was clear that he was not going to quit. Not until one of us was dead.

Grabbing his wrist as he slashed at me, I managed to turn him and plunge his arm into the water. He went under.

I twisted my body, got one leg over his shoulder, and hooked my legs around him. Still holding his wrist, I put all my weight on him, driving him deeper into the black waters.

It only took a couple of minutes before the thrashing stopped. He still had the knife in his hand when I pulled his lifeless body to the surface.

This wasn't the way I liked to end things. But he'd given me no choice.

I swam around the stern end of the yacht and climbed up onto the dock.

There was no one by the restaurants when I went back up the stairs to the parking lot. That was probably a good thing, since that wine bottle to my face had opened up a cut that was still bleeding.

"Nice look," Vaughn joked when I reached the cars. "Very manly."

"Yeah." I took a towel he grabbed out of his car and pressed it to the wound. "I'm guessing you use this rag to polish your car?"

"Exactly. But the wax is very antiseptic."

"I'm sure."

"All done? I saw Volpe's assistant making her way through the lot. She practically sprinted up the stairs toward the hotel."

I nodded. "The two bodyguards are in a boat a couple of slips in from the yacht. But you'd better get to them before they wake up. They're not going to be happy when they come to."

"No problem. And Volpe?"

"He must have fallen overboard. He had a lot to drink."

"I'll take care of things from here." He tossed me my keys.

"Tomorrow, make an anonymous call to the police. Get his sidekick arrested for sex trafficking of underage girls."

"Happy to do it, boss."

"Oh, and one more thing." I pulled the immobilizer from my pocket. "I need you to trace this device."

Vaughn cocked an eyebrow in surprise. "It's not yours?"

"Nope."

He pulled his phone from his pocket, opened an app, and ran it over the device. "Where did you find it?"

"Doesn't matter. Just find out who it was issued to."

"Can I hold onto it?"

"No."

"Okay then, boss. I'll get back to you when I know something."

Chapter Six

Avalie

I READ Reed's invitation to dinner tonight a few times, but it didn't raise any warning flags.

Luckily, I now knew his identity, his reason for being in San Clemente, and his mission.

Sitting with my feet up on the railing of the tiny balcony of my seedy little apartment, I stared down the sunlit street in the direction of his place.

I had to believe I was still okay. Aside from accidentally leaving my immobilizer behind, he'd have a very difficult time figuring out who I was. One of my many skills was that of a master hacker. Creating false digital footprints was an easy thing to do. Any record of me would be inaccessible to him from here.

To make sure that my identity was thoroughly innocent, Payam was monitoring any online searches for me today. The inquiries about my phone number or first name from Reed's IP address, which I figured he'd do, revealed that Avalie Briar did indeed reside in San Francisco. Her job description agreed with what I'd told him, and a quick check on social media displayed a network of friends and various posts, establishing my legitimacy.

Once again, I found myself going over his text. A question lingered in my mind. Why did he want to see me? I was a person who was accustomed to compartmentalizing my personal and professional life. I didn't generally do things on impulse.

Maybe he wanted to see me because of the copy of the Jane Austen book I left behind.

Or maybe he found my immobilizer and was suspicious about what the hell I was doing with it.

Maybe he really missed me, especially the great sex we had. But getting together again seemed like the desire for something more on his part. And Reed's job wasn't conducive to relationships.

In short, I was feeling a little bit wary. But I had good reason to be cautious. I couldn't afford to mess up even the tiniest bit.

I flexed my shoulders and looked over his text again. I'd find out what he wanted once I got there.

As for me wanting to see him, well, there was a saying about keeping your friends close and your enemies closer.

I responded to his message.

- *Sounds good. What time*
- *Seven?*

It was already past 4:30. It had been a late night, albeit a successful one. So I'd slept in this morning and been busy with work ever since. I needed to shower and get dressed.

- *Where?*
- *I'll come to your apartment and we can figure it out*
- *Not a good idea. I haven't forgotten about yesterday*

He texted me a smile.
- *I have my friend Pat with me. Do you mind if she comes along*
- *Not at all. How about the restaurant at San Clemente Pier*
- *Which one? Isn't there a couple*
- *We can decide when we get there*
- *Okay*
- *Looking forward to meeting Pat*

I put my phone away, thinking that maybe I shouldn't have mentioned my imaginary friend. Now, I'd have to make some excuse as to why Pat wasn't coming tonight.

I couldn't say she had to leave because of an emergency at home. Nothing like that would work. I was using the buddy system to keep him at arm's length. I had a roommate, so he couldn't come to my apartment. I also couldn't stay overnight at his place. I could just tell him I didn't want to, but my research said that thirty-something women in this decade took destination trips with their girlfriends. They hung out together and excluded males from their group activities and partying. It was best to stick with that as a cover.

Drying off after my shower was a little more painful than I expected. The side where I had been kicked by one of the attackers last night was red and sensitive to the touch. I'd broken ribs before, and this just felt like a bad bruise.

Going out into the bedroom, I pulled open the single drawer that housed everything I had.

Unlike Reed's newly purchased collection of clothes, hanging neatly in his closet, my wardrobe was sparse. I had a credit card, but my principles discouraged me from using it. Payam had clipped the number from a large corporate expense account, but it was still a stolen number. I didn't feel good about charging to it, and I wouldn't...unless it was absolutely necessary.

Based on my observations thus far in Southern California, everyone seemed to dress casually. San Clemente was a beach town, and the daywear for most women my age and younger was bathing suits with colorful wraps to wear over the bottoms. Bikini tops were in evidence on the streets and in the restaurants. At night, jeans, sundresses, t-shirts and casual tops were in vogue. I couldn't imagine that it would be any different wherever Reed was planning on having dinner.

At a thrift shop a few blocks down from where El Camino Real crossed the top of Del Mar, I'd picked up a few things to wear. One of them was a dark green sundress with delicate yellow flower patterns, and that was what I pulled out for tonight. It was pretty, but not so loud that it would draw too much attention. Glancing at myself in the mirror, I felt like I belonged here. As I went out the door, I grabbed Reed's sweatshirt and wrapped it around my waist.

The late afternoon sun was gradually making its way west toward the Pacific, but sunset was still hours off. As I stood on the sidewalk, I loved the warm feel of sunlight on my skin.

I was plenty early and considered walking back to the thrift shop, but decided they were probably closed. Exploring the beach trail and walking out on the pier was really appealing. I hadn't done that yet. Putting my feet in the ocean, with waves crashing a few yards offshore, wasn't something I could do at home. Just to feel the warm sand between my toes would be exciting. I'd wanted to do it yesterday. But unfortunately, after messaging Payam, I needed to go back to the apartment. Now that I'd met Reed, there was a lot more research that had to be done about him.

The most direct path to the beach was down Avenida Victoria, and I looked at the glimmering ocean in the distance, but that route was not in the cards. It meant passing by Reed's apartment.

So I cut across to Del Mar. The street glowed golden from the sun, and it occurred to me that this was aptly called 'happy hour'. People of all ages were wandering along the sidewalks, some carrying bags and some just idly looking in the shop windows. Surprisingly, most of the stores were still open. Small groups milled about outside of wine bars and restaurants.

As I strolled down the sidewalk, my skin warmed in the late afternoon light, and the smells of perfume and sunscreen mingled with the scent of food and sea air. This was absolutely the most beautiful downtown I'd ever seen in my entire life.

Moving down in the direction of the ocean, I walked past a group of people waiting at the trolley stop. Laughter and voices combined with music emanating from the open front of a bar. I passed the library and its bookstore where I'd met Reed. As the saying goes, I was like a kid in a candy shop.

These were sights, smells, and sounds that I hadn't experienced before. Where I came from, one either lived in a highly sanitized, privileged world or in one that was far more toxic. In both worlds, products were often scarce, and the government controlled the population and potential crime with ever-present video monitoring and swift interventions. And there was no middle ground between those worlds. It was a matter of 'haves' and 'have nots'.

It occurred to me that I hadn't seen any sign of police since I'd arrived.

Del Mar became residential beyond the library, winding down between two and three-story apartments where residents sat out on balconies with drinks in hand, relaxing and occasionally chatting with passersby. Young boys and girls on bikes and scooters and skateboards wove between pedestrians and cars and electric carts.

As I made my way around a bend in the road, a picturesque panorama suddenly unfolded before me. Palm trees rose above a parking lot and a park, and a long pier stretched out into the shimmering Pacific. My breath caught in my chest.

At the bottom of the hill, with the ocean straight ahead, Del Mar curled to the left around a line of restaurants, small hotels, and residential buildings. Opposite them, I spied people, carrying beach bags and umbrellas, standing on the platform of a working train station. Couples held the hands of small children, all of them still wearing bathing suits and oversized shirts and light sundresses.

Following a crowd, I crossed the tracks that ran north and south. I could see the rail line curving along the shoreline in both directions.

The smell of fried food wafted in the air, drawing my attention to the two restaurants that sat on either side of the entrance to the pier. And as I gazed at the scores of fishermen casting their lines off the weathered wooden planks of the quarter-mile-long structure, seagulls circled above, and their sharp cries mingled with the laughter of beachgoers.

Ahead of me, waves rose up and crashed onto a sandy beach still filled with people, despite the late hour. By the water's edge, children and adults played and swam. Farther out, dozens of surfers in black and blue and red wetsuits lined up, waiting for a wave that would hurtle them toward the shore.

I stopped by a low wall that bordered the beach and admired the surfers' seemingly fearless spirit. They were of all ages, some perhaps as young as four or five years old and some who had to be in their seventies or older. I was captivated by the energy and sense of freedom exuded by them.

Silhouetted against the canvas of the sinking sun, the surfers would choose their wave, pop up smoothly to their feet, and carve a path along the cresting water with movements that looked both graceful and daring.

As I watched, mesmerized, they simply danced on the ocean's surface. Their colorful boards left trails of spray behind them, creating art in the air. The booming sound of the waves accompanied the rhythm of their maneuvers. And as they often finished their runs toward the beach, they would suddenly spin their board away from the shore and fly into the air as the wave collapsed into churning foam beneath them. It was truly a symphonic ballet of nature and human skill.

"Have you surfed before?"

Reed's voice startled me. I'd been too distracted to see or hear him approach.

"No, I haven't. Have you?" I asked, watching his profile. He seemed to be fascinated with them, as well. He was wearing a black short-sleeved knit shirt, khaki pants, and a pair of sandals. When he turned to answer, his eyes were hidden behind his sunglasses.

"Yes."

"Are you any good at it?"

"I could show you." He smiled. "In fact, the folks I'm renting my apartment from have some spare boards we can use. If you're up for it."

I noticed on his left cheek an inch-long cut and bruising around it. "How did you get that? It looks painful."

"Ran into a wall this afternoon, texting you."

I touched the edge of the cut but quickly drew back my hand. The gesture suddenly seemed too intimate.

"I don't think so. This cut isn't brand new. It must have happened last night."

"So, you're a doctor too?"

"No, but I'm hell with a first-aid kit."

He laughed. "Why is that? Do you get bumps and bruises often?"

I smiled. "Deflecting again. Why don't you answer me?"

"Okay, I admit it. I was starting to text you last night, then debated whether it was too soon. While I was thinking about it, the corner of a wall in the apartment leaped out at my face."

Bullshit. I knew a bruise from a fight when I saw one. If I was an expert at anything, it was that. And for one thing, the angle of the cut was wrong to have been caused by a horizontal wall corner. It was a fight, for sure. The question of who Reed had been in a fight with was something I'd like to know.

"Well, I'm glad you texted me this afternoon. By the way, I brought your sweatshirt." I started to unwrap it from around my waist, but he took hold of my hands.

"Hang on to it. It suits you. Plus, you might need it tonight. The temperature tends to drop after the sun sets." He let go of me and held up the light jacket he was holding. "I came prepared."

"Okay. Thanks."

"So, where's your roommate?" he asked. "Pat, wasn't it?"

I glanced out at the surfers as a daredevil who was close to the pier suddenly angled her board and shot between the rows of wooden pilings and out the other side. "Did you see that?"

"Yeah, right under the sign that warns surfers not to do it."

I smiled at him. "She's a rebel, I guess."

He scoffed. "So, your roommate?"

"Pat didn't want to be a fifth wheel."

"That's too bad. I was looking forward to meeting her."

I reached into my jacket pocket. "I can call her and ask her again, if you want."

"No. It's fine. I like it this way."

"Well, don't get used to it. It's our girl time, don't forget. And boys are *not* invited."

He laughed. "By the way, I accidentally left your book at my apartment.

"Accidently, hmm?" I cocked an eyebrow, letting a smile lift the corner of my lips. This was good. I needed to get back into his apartment to retrieve my immobilizer.

"Totally. But since you came on your own tonight, I'm thinking maybe you'd want to pick it up after we eat. What do you think?"

"That's a lot of thinking."

"I'm a thoughtful guy."

"You certainly are."

He glanced at the clock high on a tower above the lifeguard building. "Want to walk on the beach or out on the pier before we eat?"

"I'd like that, but I'm starving," I admitted truthfully. "I haven't eaten at all today."

"No worries. We can eat first. If you want to, we can always take a walk later."

He pointed at the restaurants on the pier, and we made our way over there.

As charming as Reed was, I needed to exercise caution around him. He wasn't merely an agent on assignment; his connections ran deep with the company's directors. This was precisely why I was here. I was targeting him and the job at the same time.

We walked up onto the pier, and the restaurant on our right had weathered shingles and colorful umbrellas for outdoor seating. The aroma of freshly grilled seafood coming from the open doors was enticing. At the tables outside and the horseshoe-shaped bar inside, the clink of dishes and glasses and the conversations of diners enjoying their meals were lively. The friendly, casual ambiance of the place blended perfectly with the coastal vibe I was getting.

To our left, a more upscale eatery had panoramic windows and outdoor seating with equally breathtaking views of the ocean. The sound of soft laughter emanated from there, hinting at a cozy, intimate atmosphere.

"Let me see where we can get a seat first."

As Reed vanished into one of the restaurants, I watched the people strolling past. It was a diverse group. In just a few moments, I saw older people dressed up for a night out, younger folks in shorts and t-shirts jogging the length of the pier, women wearing head scarves and walking arm-in-arm with small children running in front of them, and Asian-featured families pulling wagons filled with fishing gear.

Leaning against the pier's wooden railing with a dozen other idlers, I basked in the warm glow of the descending sun.

The breathtaking coastal landscape, the outdoor lifestyle, the mild climate, and the sense of community, all combined to paint a picture of a place where families could settle and live out their lives happily. Reflecting on what I'd done last night—stopping the robbery—I felt a small sense of satisfaction. Even so, I knew I hadn't done all that I needed to do to preserve a certain family. Not yet, anyway.

"We have a table on that side," Reed said, coming up behind me and gesturing towards the more upscale of the two restaurants.

As we navigated through a crowd of waiting customers, Reed pulled me close to his side, and the slight pressure of his hand against my bruised ribs made me wince involuntarily. Unfortunately, he noticed.

"What's wrong?"

"Nothing."

I shook my head and trailed after the hostess as she guided us to our table outside. Our table gave us a view of the ocean on the south side of the pier. A few hundred yards along the shore, a pedestrian bridge crossed over the railroad tracks. Near it, a large number of surfers were grouped up in the water. Even from a distance, I could tell that the waves were larger there than the ones on the north side of the pier.

Once we were seated, a server promptly appeared, taking our orders for drinks and appetizers. When she was gone, Reed pulled off his sunglasses and leaned forward, reaching across the table to hold my hand.

"How did you get that bruise on your ribs?"

Beneath the furrowed brows, there was concern in his eyes. The contrast between the person I knew him to be and the caring expression I could see on his face now was significant. He seemed genuinely worried, but he still had no clue as to who I really was.

"I ran into a wall while I was answering your text."

"No, you didn't."

"Says the man who doesn't pay attention to where he's walking." I freed my hand and touched his cheek just below the bruise.

"Fair enough." He leaned back. "As long as you're okay."

"I'm perfectly fine. No worries whatsoever."

"By the way, have any more of your girlfriends shown up?"

"Not yet. But tomorrow is another day."

Our server arrived with our drinks and assured us that the appetizers were on their way.

"So, what did you and Pat do this morning?"

I wrapped my hand around the cold drink but resisted taking a sip until I had some food in my belly. He wasn't giving up. Was it possible that he was doubting her existence?

"The things girlfriends do when they haven't seen each other for a year," I said. "We talked. What did you do?"

"Some business calls. Went for a run. Straightened up the apartment with the hope that someone would be coming by."

He paused, leaned back in his chair, and reached into his pocket.

"Oh..." He took something out and placed it on the table between us.

I stared at my immobilizer. He'd found the weapon.

"This was wedged between the cushions of the sofa. Is it yours?"

Chapter Seven

Reed

I suppose it was *nurture* and not *nature* that bred mistrust in me.

Losing my mother when I was just ten years old forced me to grow up fast. With my father being in the military and my brother significantly older, I found myself navigating through life's challenges without support.

However, perhaps it wasn't solely the absence of family that shaped me but later, the nature of my profession. Doing what I did for over a decade did manage to instill in me a constant skepticism. It was essential for survival in my line of work. The trait led me to question everything, search for clues, and identify dishonesty when confronted with it.

In that moment, Avalie's split-second pause was long enough for me to know that whatever she said next in way of explanation would be a lie.

"Yes, yes. That's mine. What a relief! I'm so glad you found it."

I'd expected her to deny that it was hers, but I realized she had to be prepared for my question.

She reached across the table to grab it, but I placed my hand on top of hers. I knew well enough the damage this little device could do. In the hands of someone who knew how to use it, the weapon could stun and immobilize a man my size for hours.

And if this weapon was synced with her biometrics, she could activate and use it on me right now. If she did, this restaurant would be closed by the time I regained consciousness.

"Can I have it?"

I gazed into her large, dark eyes and recalled my phone call with Vaughn an hour ago. There was no record of this unit in the databases he'd checked, which meant that it was contraband.

Division devices—including the immobilizers—were calibrated specifically to the assigned agent and activated only by biometric identification. Technically, no one else could operate them. It was common knowledge, however, that there were hackers capable of pirating the device codes and resetting them for unauthorized use. There were laws established to prohibit the trade or sale of them, and the punishments were stiff. But that didn't stop it from happening.

"Do you mind?" Her tone was noticeably cooler.

The moment of reckoning had arrived. Should I trust her? Was she unaware of the capabilities of this device, or was she playing a game with me? Regardless, the only way to find out was to at least pretend that I had no idea what the device was.

"Good thing I didn't toss it," I said, withdrawing my hand. "What is it?"

"I have no idea. When I found it, I thought it was a whistle, but the tube is blocked." She held it up. "The thing doesn't seem to do anything. It's a mystery, but I'm going to figure it out. It might just be my lucky charm."

"Maybe. Where did you find it?"

"I stepped on it in San Francisco, on the street right in front of the old chocolate factory. I figured a tourist must have dropped it."

"Huh." I tried to sound only mildly interested. "How long ago was that?"

She shrugged. "I don't know. Maybe a month ago."

I chuckled. "And do you keep *everything* you find on the street?"

"Only when they're as interesting and mysterious as this thing." She smiled, a hint of mischief in her eyes. "And I don't limit myself to things. Sometimes people fall into that category too. Like the ones I find at sidewalk book sales. Occasionally, that works out pretty well."

"I guess that thing *is* a lucky charm."

Beneath the table, she brushed a bare foot up against my ankle, and my mind immediately drifted back to the image of her naked body stretched out on my bed. Sex with her had been fucking amazing. Judging by the slight blush that tinged the tips of her ears and her cheeks, I decided that she was thinking the same thing.

As our server approached with the appetizers, Avalie pocketed the device and smiled at the young woman. A plate of oysters was placed before each of us, and she wasted no time diving in.

Watching her eat was both fascinating and arousing. She was so deliberate in the way that she first put a generous dollop of horseradish and a spritz of lemon on each oyster on the plate. As she did so, she examined each shell carefully, apparently admiring the pale, delicate colors of the satin-smooth insides and the glistening treasures they held. The anticipation was palpable as she brought three oysters in succession to her full lips, closing her eyes slightly and savoring the blend of flavors in each one.

As I watched her mouth, my arousal sharpened at the memory of the softness of it.

"Now I understand why they say oysters are aphrodisiacs," I mused quietly as I downed my first oyster.

Her eyes lifted to my face, and there was a playful glint in them. "In that case, you should have ordered something else."

"And why is that?"

"Well," she said quietly. "I don't think you need any help with your sexual performance."

I stretched out my legs and adjusted my tightening khakis. "Same to you."

She lifted her drink and took a sip, watching me intently over the rim.

I pushed my plate away. "Can we pack the rest of these oysters and order dinner to go?"

"Absolutely not. I told you already about my roommate. She's expecting me back." Her gaze shifted to the remaining oysters on my plate. "Aren't you going to finish those?"

I swapped my plate with hers. "Ask and it shall be yours."

"Only oysters? Or other things too?"

"I'm known to be a good guy. You'll never know unless you ask."

The change of expression on her face, the fleeting moment of contemplation, gave me another reminder that there was a whole lot going on in that pretty head that I wasn't privy to.

She nodded. "I'll remember that when the time comes."

The waitress returned a minute later, asking if we were ready to place our order. Where I came from, the luxury of indulging in fresh seafood had become a distant memory. Because of the pollution, all the food was sourced from carefully monitored fish farms. Avalie ordered one of the day's seafood specials, and I followed suit.

As we waited for our meal, we chatted about San Clemente. From where we sat, we could see the house built by the town's developer. Casa Romantica was perched on a bluff overlooking the pier and the beaches.

"Did you know that the town was built during Prohibition?" I asked, wondering how well she knew the history.

Avalie paused, toying for a moment with her silverware and lining them up in a row in front of her.

"No, I didn't." She fixed her gaze attentively on my face. "It's pretty impressive how much you know about this area. Are you sure you didn't work around here in high school or college? I can definitely see you as one of those lifeguards up in the tower."

I shook my head. The truth was that I had a love-and-hate relationship with my job. The love part was that I delved into the history of the places where the job took me. And not just the facts and figures, but the social and cultural history. Who these people were and what the future might hold for them. The hate part was that I was an assassin.

"I like researching the places where I have to spend time."

"A history buff."

"I guess so. I see history as a living thing. The smallest event can shape the future of a place and its people."

"That's an interesting way to look at things. So you don't think it's the great social currents of a time that affect the future?" she asked.

"That's certainly part of it, I suppose. But I believe those currents are often shaped by small, often unrecorded actions of individuals who never make it into the history books."

"But so many people work hard to live in a way that doesn't affect others. They hide away, living in quiet obscurity. What about them?" Avalie asked.

"I guess that's true. Some people do intentionally try to

conceal their actions, but those actions still cast an influence on the future."

"I don't get that," she protested.

"Okay. Consider San Clemente, for example. Why was the town built right here? Why build this pier in this location, rather than a few miles north in Dana Point, where there was a natural harbor, a small fishing village, and a couple of tourist hotels a mile away in San Juan Capistrano?"

"Tell me, why?" she asked.

"Because the handful of men who were behind the plan to build this town wanted a spot sixty miles north of San Diego and sixty miles south of Los Angeles, far from law enforcement. It was the perfect location to build a place where they could land cases of smuggled liquor."

"Liquor?" she questioned.

"It was a big business in the 1920s. Prohibition made it a federal offense to sell alcohol in the United States. Look at this coastline. No harbor. Just this wide-open ocean."

Avalie gazed at the pier and the endless vista of water, then shifted her gaze to the buildings all along the shore. "But look at this place. Building an entire town is a world away from living a life in obscurity."

"I believe those men—most of them, anyway—saw the town as a screen they could hide behind. It was really the pier they wanted," I explained.

"I'm disappointed. I thought they built this dock for people to fish off."

I laughed. "Nope. And not for the kids to surf under, either."

"Who did they think they were, undercover Al Capones?" she asked.

"Close. Bankers and judges and politicians."

As she considered this, she formed a triangle with her utensils, with one point of the shape directed at me. "And they broke the law in order to make a good life for themselves, their families, and those who moved here to establish roots."

"They did break the law." I shrugged. "But Prohibition was widely unpopular, for the most part. In fact, if you look up there..." I pointed at a sprawling house on the bluff directly over the pier. Its white walls and red-tiled roof glowed in the light. "Ole Hanson, the primary developer, had his office in that octagonal room up there in his house so that he could see when the shipments were coming in."

"He saw an opportunity and he took it. You said yourself Prohibition was widely unpopular," she insisted.

"They built a town to hide an illegal, money-making enterprise. They were rogues and rebels."

"History is full of rogues and rebels. They bring about change. They make life exciting, worth living," she argued. "So what if their initial motivation was questionable? They built this beautiful village that we're still enjoying today. I think that's valuable."

"You're determined to be their fan, aren't you?"

"I cheer for people. Especially those who go against the system to leave their mark, to make a difference, even to live happily ever after. So long as they don't hurt others and keep to themselves."

"Well, there was no happily-ever-after for Hanson. In the 1930s, when Prohibition was repealed, the Depression cleaned him out. With no cash flowing in from liquor, the town mostly went bankrupt. Hanson lost almost everything and moved back to Los Angeles."

She sighed as she looked up at the colorful array of buildings on the hills overlooking the ocean. Windows flashed brilliantly colored reflections of the setting sun.

"I'm glad the town survived." Avalie lowered her gaze and looked directly into my eyes. "Some things are worth saving.

Erase Me

They can end up having value even if they start off wrong. *Even if someone breaks the rules.*"

Our dinner arrived, and as we ate, our conversation wandered from the architecture of the town's original buildings to the surfers to the weather. She mentioned that she'd seen a poster in a window on Del Mar today advertising an art festival down here by the pier this weekend.

"Will you be around then?" I had to ask.

"I don't know yet. We have our apartment until Saturday, but I'm only planning one day at a time."

While we were finishing dessert, we were treated to an art show put on by Nature.

To the west, an amazing sunset over the Pacific unfolded, streaking the sky with a breathtaking spectacle of reds and yellows. Around us, the atmosphere changed. The entire 'Pier Bowl', as the locals called this part of town, was suddenly imbued with a sense of awe. Customers in the restaurant, people gathered on the pier, and those still on the beach all seemed caught up in the need to capture the moment with their phones and cameras.

Avalie and I, however, appeared to be the only people who weren't engrossed in documenting the scene. Instead, I watched her as she silently soaked in the natural beauty. The effects of the colors and the light on the land, the sea, and the sky were simply magical. And like me, she was completely detached from the digital frenzy around us.

I broke the silence. "I'm impressed."

"Me, too. I don't think I've ever seen a view more beautiful than this."

I was about to mention San Francisco and its equally stunning sunsets, but the words died on my tongue.

Fuck me, but she was so beautiful.

The sun's golden rays bathed her face, emphasizing the delicate contours and casting a mesmerizing glow on her features. Her eyes, reflecting the colors of the sky, projected a depth that mirrored the beauty of the scene before us. I'd thought Avalie was beautiful from the first moment I saw her. But in this particular moment, she was a living canvas painted by the hand of Nature itself.

This kind of reaction while on assignment was not helpful.

Still, I said, "I was talking about you. I'm impressed by *you*."

She opened her mouth to respond but then closed it. The blush on her cheeks deepened as our eyes locked.

"I mean, your phone isn't glued to your hand."

She laughed and then looked away, drawing a deep breath of the sea air. "I spend enough hours in front of a screen for work. I love it when I'm out of the house and can feel, smell, enjoy Nature. This is a gift."

Our server came back to offer more coffee.

"But I don't see you snapping videos or pictures, either," Avalie said. "Or checking headline news or box scores."

"No. That's not me. Whatever is meant to happen will happen without me refereeing from the sidelines."

Again, that look crossed her face. It came with that momentary pause as if she were analyzing me rather than having a conversation with me. But none of that bothered me. I was enjoying the play of light and shadow that highlighted the gentle curve of her smile and the graceful lines of her face.

Damn, but I was definitely drawn to her. Again, not helpful.

"Maybe it's time for us to exchange our last names," I suggested.

"Briar. Avalie Briar."

This matched with the information I gathered during my internet searches today.

"Reed Michael." I stretched out my hand, and she didn't hesitate to place her hand in mine. Her fingers were cold. "I'm glad your friend Pat decided not to come to dinner."

"Me too."

"What do you think she's doing now?"

"I don't know. But she's a big girl, and there's plenty to do around San Clemente."

"Do you have time to walk on the beach before you need to head back?"

"For a bit. I can't stay too long."

"What's on the agenda for tomorrow?"

"I'm not sure. I need to check with her."

"Well, as you said, there's plenty to do around San Clemente," I reminded her.

"And I need to see if anyone else is coming."

"Right."

"What did you have in mind?" she asked.

"How about surfing?"

"I told you, I don't know how."

"I'll teach you."

"Don't you have to work tomorrow?" she asked.

"Work can wait. What do you say?"

Maybe it was the device in her pocket and the fact that I wasn't happy with her answer, or maybe it was the realization that the background check I did on her today yielded surprisingly clean results, or maybe I just wanted to spend time with her. Regardless of my true motivation, I realized I was pressing her.

"Okay. Let's do it."

I was relieved.

By the time we left the restaurant, the sun had already dipped into the Pacific Ocean, but the wisps of clouds continued to color the sky with every imaginable shade. Avalie and I strolled along the palm tree-lined path that ran between the beach and the railroad tracks.

She was looking ahead at the beach near the overhead pedestrian bridge. "Funny. The light is starting to fade, but the beach is still crowded. Actually, I think more surfers are getting into the water than are leaving."

"Yeah, I was reading about that in a surf magazine that was left in my apartment. This beach is called 'T-Street'. According to the article, it's a busy place all year round, but night surfing is really popular at this time of the year."

"Night surfing? Really? That sounds kind of dangerous. Don't they worry about sharks?"

"I guess not."

"But why do they do it? What's so special about surfing at night?" Her eyes were scanning the water. "The waves look the same."

"It's because of the blue bioluminescence. The phenomenon is back in Southern California right now."

"What's that?" she asked.

"It's a glow caused by tiny organisms that undergo a chemical reaction in the water. It happens when they're agitated by the surf, or by the wake from a boat, or they're churned up by a protruding reef. They emit a neon blue light. It's pretty amazing. It's not dark enough to see it right now, but it will be in an hour."

"My God, you're a walking encyclopedia when it comes to Southern California. The history, the marine life..."

"That's because I'm from New York. We don't get to experience things like bioluminescence on the East Coast." I gestured towards the beach. "Besides, I like being here and knowing more about the town and the culture. That's true about every place I go. It's a perk of the job."

"You mean, your job in property insurance," she said.

"Right. Property insurance," I repeated.

There was that look again that made me feel like I was being analyzed.

"You said it's back. The blue bioluminescence. It comes and goes?"

"From what I hear, it shows up for a short time between March and June and then again in the fall."

"That's pretty cool. I didn't expect to experience any of this." She stopped and gazed at the surfers in the fading light. "Do you need to be a good athlete to surf?"

I'd seen all of her, and Avalie was strong. She had a lean athletic build. At the same time, she was sexy, with curves in all the right places. I tore my gaze away from her body and watched a trio of surfers go by us onto the beach. She wasn't coming back to my place tonight, so I had to get my head out of the gutter.

"How strong a swimmer are you?" I asked.

"Mediocre."

"Flexible?"

"My joints have been known to creak on occasion."

"What do you do for cardio?" I asked.

"Does going from my laptop to the fridge count?"

I smiled. "Balance?"

"Not great." She made a face and touched a spot on her rib. "Here's the proof."

"How patient are you when it comes to learning new things?"

She scoffed. "Not exactly a strong point. My parents told me I gave up on riding a bicycle after the first try because I didn't master it right off."

I stopped, facing her. "You can't ride a bicycle?"

"I can now. But it took years before I got back to it." She linked her arm in mine, and we started walking again.

"That doesn't sound too promising."

"You're not going to back out on me now, are you?"

I laughed. "Hey, you can't scare me with all that stuff. We're surfing tomorrow. We'll just warn the lifeguards in advance."

"Excellent. What time?"

A woman, pushing a double stroller and holding the hand of

a third young child, cut us off and jerked to a stop in front of us. I immediately recognized her. She was the one ready to fight Avalie for the Jane Austen book at the library book sale yesterday.

"Oh good. People I know," she said in a rush. "Can you watch these two while I'll take this one to the bathroom?"

She didn't wait for an answer. Leaving the stroller in front of us, she scooped up the other child and ran to the nearby bathroom building.

"What just happened?" Avalie asked.

I had no chance to answer, for both children in the stroller started screaming simultaneously.

Chapter Eight

Avalie

The younger child was screaming the loudest, and I recognized her as the one riding on her mother's back yesterday. Seemed like she was holding some kind of grudge against me.

"Look, sweetie. I don't have the book. Seriously, I don't. He's got it," I explained, glancing toward the bathroom. These two were crying for their mother, but she was nowhere in sight.

Feeling kind of useless, I crouched in front of the stroller, grabbing each of their small hands. The older one, after giving me a serious look, switched from wailing to whining, throwing in an occasional *Mama!* for good measure. Meanwhile, the younger child—her cheeks flushed red—took a deep breath, like she was gearing up for something.

Then, everything went quiet as she held her breath. Her chest was puffed up as if she was going to blow the world apart with the next exhalation. Seconds crawled by, and I felt a panicky heat rise into my face.

"Hey, she's not breathing," I blurted out, glancing up at Reed.

"She's just holding her breath," he said, leaning in for a closer look.

"Just? *Just?*"

If this was some normal behavior for children, I had no idea. I was way out of the loop on that topic. And judging from Reed's perplexed expression, he was no child-rearing expert either.

The toddler's flushed face turned to a shade of red that rivaled the sunset colors. Veins bulged on her forehead.

"What should we do?" I scanned our surroundings, desperately seeking help. Though there were plenty of people on the beach—and many families—none were paying the slightest attention to us.

"No clue," Reed admitted, his tone as urgent as my own.

The older devil-child was grinning, obviously enjoying the show. Her gaze kept switching from her sister to us and back.

What if this one burst a blood vessel in her head? What if a lung imploded? Years ago, I did take an emergency medical technology course. Not that I could remember much of it now when it mattered. In fact, I don't recall anything in the course being of any use right now.

I couldn't wait any longer. I unbuckled the stroller's seatbelt and scooped the distressed toddler up into my arms. As I did, the little monster expelled her breath in a gush. And it was a good thing she did because I was about to start pounding on her back. I'd just remembered that was one of the methods for resuscitation.

"Okay, that's good. Now breathe," I encouraged her. "Like this."

Taking deep, exaggerated breaths myself, I started making ridiculous sounds. Dramatically, I filled my cheeks and then puffed them out like a pair of balloons. She watched me. The red faded from her cheeks, and her face creased into a delighted smile as she pressed my cheeks and I complied with a sound like a truck horn as the air escaped.

She laughed, and so did her sister in the stroller.

That was how their mother and older sister found us when they came emerged from the bathroom. The child ran toward us, shouting.

"What's funny?"

"Her." The one in the stroller pointed at me.

When the young mother reached us, I couldn't hold back my frustration. "That was ridiculous. How could you leave your children out here with total strangers?"

"You weren't strangers," she said, looking surprised. "We met before."

"We didn't meet. You don't know my name or his name." I gestured to Reed. The child in my arms continued to playfully slap my cheek, and I continued to perform for her as I glared at the mother. "We could have been...could have been..."

"I'm Tina."

"What?"

"I'm Tina. And these are my three little trolls. That's us, Tina and the Trolls. And that's my husband Brandon over there, waiting for his wave." She motioned vaguely toward one of the two or three dozen surfers sitting on their boards.

Why didn't she ask him? I thought. Or just take the other two into the bathroom with her?

The idea of someone stealing these precious babies was terrifying. These thoughts and a bunch more were about to explode out of me, but Reed interrupted.

"Nice to meet you, Tina. I'm Reed and this is Avalie."

"So glad I ran into you. You were a lifesaver. I didn't bring a change of clothes for this one." She gave a side glance to her daughter, standing beside her. "And trust me, that was an emergency."

"Still, you didn't know us. We could have been a couple of weirdos," I protested, attempting to hand the child back to her mother. But the little troublemaker clung to my neck, even pressing a sloppy mouth against my cheek before finally letting go.

"Look, she even gave you a kiss," she chirped. "She doesn't usually do that, believe me."

Tina probably said that to everyone she palmed off her children to.

I wasn't one to get flustered, but to be honest, the sweetness of the moment actually got to me. I plunked the tricky troll into her mother's arms.

"I understand where you're coming from." She leaned down, placing her baby in the stroller and buckling her in. "But this is a small town. Everyone knows each other. I've practically known half the parents on this beach since high school. It's all about community, watching out for each other, and taking care of everyone's kids."

"You could have asked one of them. At least, someone you really know."

"And besides," she continued, ignoring my comment. "You like Jane Austen. I like Jane Austen. So I knew you had to be okay."

"That is got to be the sketchiest reasoning for leaving your precious—"

"Trolls." She laughed. "Oh, by the way, are you done with the book yet? I still need to read it for my book club."

She was so confidently at ease with herself that I couldn't help myself. "Yes, you can have it. Where can I leave it for you?"

First, I had to get it back from Reed, though.

She rattled off her address, which she said was walking distance from here. I told her I'd try to drop it off at her door sometime in the next few days.

Erase Me

The oldest child ran off across the beach toward the water, and Tina maneuvered the stroller off the walking path and onto the sand. By the time we parted ways, you would have thought we were best friends.

The last blush of sunset was fading, and darkness was rapidly approaching. Despite this, no one was ready to leave the beach.

Reed and I climbed the first dozen steps to a landing on the pedestrian bridge that connected T-Street Beach to the neighborhood on the bluff. From up here, we could observe the surfers' maneuvers. I enjoyed seeing Tina's younger children toddling barefoot in and out of the water.

Mixed in with the men and women out of the water, I noticed quite a few teenagers and some surprisingly young surfers riding the waves.

"How early do you think they start teaching their kids to surf?" I asked Reed.

"I wouldn't be surprised if Tina's older one is already a surfer. Look at her," Reed said, nodding towards the child.

A surfboard lay in the sand, and she was stretched out on top of it. As I watched, she made a smooth, lightning-quick movement from lying on the board to a standing position. As she got her feet under her, she crouched slightly, her body completely balanced. She was a mirror image of the surfers out on the water.

"She's practicing her pop-up. This helps improve speed and efficiency in getting up on the board once in the water. You'll be doing plenty of that tomorrow."

"That looks sort of difficult."

He smiled. "You can handle it."

As we lingered there, Tina's words resonated deeply. Conversations were going on between groups sitting in the sand. They all seemed to know each other. A small gathering had formed around a blazing fire pit, and the smell of wood smoke and the ocean was intoxicating. Nearby, boxes of pizza were being delivered. There was enough food there alone to feed half the surfing families on the beach. What had been a lively volleyball game now broke up with the fading light, and the players and onlookers now joined the pizza crew and the fire pit group.

Standing with Reed, I saw a vibrant community spirit. The constant crash and wash of the waves only underscored what was clearly a deeply felt connection between the sea and the residents.

Contemplating what I had gleaned about this town before arriving and comparing it to my current experience, I realized that San Clemente truly lived up to its reputation. This town was a happy place, a haven for families. Along with the slower, beach town lifestyle—'chill' was the way a store clerk on Del Mar had described it—the place had a community fabric in which family and surfing were woven together. I'd heard that description repeated many times over the years, and the truth of it now resonated clearly.

"Again, I'm impressed," Reed said, turning to me.

"I'm starting to think you're easily impressed."

"No. I mean it."

"Okay, I'll bite. Impressed about what?"

"How you handled that situation." He was looking down at Tina and her trolls, now standing with friends by the fire pit. Her husband, still in his wetsuit, was bringing slices of pizza over to them.

I shook my head. "That was hardly a crisis. Those two little troublemakers were just playing games with us."

His hand reached for mine and held it. "You handled it like a natural. Do you have much experience with children?"

I scoffed. "None whatsoever."

Being a loner pretty much summed up my life. There were no large family get-togethers. No gatherings around a beach fire. There was nothing like this. There was only the constant fear of being caught, and I couldn't see any shift from this down the road.

"No sisters or brothers?"

"No, I'm an only child." Turning the question around, I asked, "How about you? Any experience with children?"

"I'm an expert, can't you tell?" came the sarcastic response.

Playfully tugging on his arm, I asked, "Time for the truth. Any siblings?"

He paused for a moment before answering, "I have an older brother and twin half-sisters."

"Wow, I never would have guessed. Are you close to them?"

He responded with a nonchalant shrug, "How do you describe close?"

"Do you see them? Talk to them? Do you get together, at all?"

"My brother and I work all the time. Trying to find the time that works for everyone is always a challenge." Something softened in his expression. "But we like each other. I especially get along with my half-sisters."

"Half, how?"

"My father married again after my mother passed away."

I knew about Reed's family before arriving in San Clemente and I'd learned even more today. The emotional side of him and the openness about his family caught me off guard, though. His honesty was unexpected.

"I'm so sorry about your mother. When did that happen?"

"Years ago."

"But you have memories of her?"

"Sure. I was ten when she died."

Regardless of how I felt, not having a large family, I appreciated having my parents around. Even though society emphasized the value of extensive family ties, I knew that the quality of our connection mattered more than the quantity of hypothetical siblings or cousins.

"Did you lose your mother in an accident?"

"Cancer." His jaws clenched, and he let go of my hand, leaning on the metal railing and gazing into the darkness for a moment. When he turned his face back, his expression had become passive, impenetrable.

Emotions he'd allowed me to glimpse of his loss were now under control. The softness that had surfaced briefly was now gone. What was left was a guarded expression that showed no hint of the pain he still carried. And then, even that defensive look disappeared. The easy-going Reed had returned.

"Look, the night surfers are making their runs," he announced, watching the waves.

It was now quite dark. Stars were beginning to light up the sky, looking like shimmering diamonds against the deep blue.

The families with kids were nearly all gone, and the diehard surfers who remained were wearing colorful glow-in-the-dark necklaces, wristbands, and anklets. Even their surfboards were trimmed with them. I looked for my new friend Tina. She and her children were gone, too.

"What's the difference between day and night surfing?" I asked Reed.

"During the day, you obviously have better visibility. You can see the waves, gauge their size, shape, and direction more easily."

"I assume that's crucial for beginners."

"For sure. And it's also important because you have more eyes on you."

"Making sure I don't drown," I said with a wry smile.

"Exactly."

"So, what's the draw about night surfing?" I asked.

"The thrill, I suppose," Reed admitted. "But there's also a meditative, Zen quality to it. You're out there in the darkness, sometimes by yourself. There's no boundary between the ocean and the huge canopy of sky above you. You can hear the waves breaking on the shore, but you're almost protected sitting on your board out beyond them. And the swells rise and fall beneath you lifting you up and easing you down. It's a powerful feeling."

I poked him in the chest. "Until a shark takes a big bite right here."

He moved quickly, and before I knew it, he had me in a tight embrace. His speed and strength were impressive. I'd started this. But still, the sudden closeness took me by surprise. And, even more surprising, it felt so natural.

I liked Reed, more than I wanted to.

But he knew nothing about me. He knew nothing about all the ways that I was planning to work against him. I would challenge him, fight him, even kill him if I had to. In this situation, there were no rules of fair play. Honesty played no role.

It had to be that way. I had to win.

Even with all that in mind, Reed's strong embrace felt like a shield. It was ironic, but it made me feel safe in the face of the chaos I knew was coming. Chaos I would be responsible for.

But despite all that, in this moment, everything outside faded away. It was just the two of us in our own little world.

"Thank you for ditching your friend and coming out with me."

I was on the verge of making a wiseass remark and pulling away.

I needed to create some distance before this transformed into something romantic. The thought of having sex with someone you might have to kill in the next couple of days just seemed a bit awkward. I wasn't going back to his place. Now that I knew who he was, we weren't going to have sex again. Ever.

But our gazes met, and I found myself leaning closer. The

night air surrounded us, and the sea breeze and the sound of waves filled my senses. He gently cupped the side of my head, tilting it, his mouth brushing over mine.

The spark between us was so damn perfect. I must have made a sound that he took as permission. Maybe it was. He kissed me hungrily, exploring my mouth.

I felt the pressure building inside me, and I broke off the kiss.

"Reed...I have to get back," I murmured.

"I know. I can't think straight when I'm with you," he confessed, leaning his forehead against mine. "When can I see you again?"

"You're going to teach me to surf tomorrow. Remember?"

"Oh, yeah. Tomorrow. Do we have to wait that long?"

I smiled, pulling out of his arms. Just then, a voice called out from the road beyond the metal footbridge above us.

"I still got it. Your bag. I'm keeping it."

The darkness concealed the speaker, but we both knew who it was. The strange man in the parking lot off Del Mar.

"What's that about?" I asked him. "What's the big deal about this bag?"

Reed shook his head and led me back down the steps to the beach trail. "I have no idea, but I'm not going to worry about it."

From the frown he cast up toward the bluff, though, I could see he wasn't entirely happy.

Chapter Nine

Reed

THE MIDDAY SUN cast a brilliant glow over Doheny Beach in Dana Point, painting a picturesque scene along the Southern California coastline. The sky was a vibrant blue, unblemished by clouds, and the air was filled with the invigorating scent of saltwater.

Standing in the warm, white sand by the water's edge, I took in the view of beaches, bluffs, and shimmering water all the way to the pier in San Clemente. To my right, the manmade breakwater for the Dana Point marina offered a perfect stretch of beach for a beginner surfer like Avalie.

Right now, there were surfers on their boards for as far as I could see, but there was a small congregation of newbies close to where we were.

We'd agreed to meet up outside my place this morning, and Avalie showed up with a borrowed skin suit from one of her neighbors. I drove us over from San Clemente in my car with our surfboards strapped to the top.

For the next hour, she'd been a rockstar of a student, totally acing all the warm-ups I threw at her on the beach. I think she must have practiced the pop-up move after seeing that little girl do it at the beach last night because she did that with the agility of a martial arts professional.

"I needed that break," she called out, her bare feet sinking into the sand as she strode over from the state park restrooms.

"What do you say we try catching a wave?"

"Definitely."

I strapped the board's leash around my ankle, and she watched me.

"Oh, I was wondering. Why come to Dana Point? It's only a couple of miles from San Clemente. But that beach where we were last night, T-Street, why not go there?"

"The long, consistent break of the waves here is perfect for novices. Plus, with fewer people spread over a wide area, there's a reduced chance of collisions."

"I spent an hour going through all those exercises, and you still call me a novice?" She smiled.

"Let's see what you got." I picked up my surfboard. "Ready?"

Once she had the leash secured around her ankle, Avalie picked up the board and stood studying the breaking waves. If I didn't already know she was new to the sport and that everything she knew was from our morning lesson, one might have mistaken her for an expert ready to deliver some ass-kicking runs.

"Competitive, aren't you?"

"You could tell?" She smiled.

We waded into the water, and the light, quartering, offshore breeze made for excellent surfing.

"First things first. Let's paddle out and get comfortable on the board." I stretched out on my board and showed her the paddling technique, lifting my head as my arms pulled me through the water.

She followed my movements, staying at my side. We weren't far from the shore when a wave crashed over her head. She surfaced, smiling.

"Paddling is crucial. It gets you out to the surf break, the zone where we pick our wave and take off. Just remember, slow and steady to start," I told her. "The fast, hard paddling comes when we take the wave."

Avalie nodded and followed my lead.

"Now, once we're out there, it's all about positioning. See those swells and the waves forming in the distance? We want to catch one just as it starts to peak," I explained, pointing to a set of waves coming in.

"How do I know which one to go for?"

"You watch the approaching swells. You want to catch a wave before it gets too steep. Wait for one that's just starting to form, and when you decide to go, paddle hard and pop up on the board."

We sat on our boards, Avalie studying the waves, and I couldn't help but watch her. With her wet hair slicked back and her face lit with excitement, she was absolutely stunning.

"Here comes one," she called out, drawing my attention seaward.

As the wave reached us, I gave her a gentle push as she paddled. A moment later, she stood up, attempting to find her balance. The wave lifted her, and for a few seconds, she rode the surface before pitching sideways off the board.

She was laughing hard when she surfaced. "Well, that didn't go as planned."

"No worries! That was a great first effort. You'll get the hang of it. Let's paddle back out and try again."

I figured it would probably take her a dozen or more tries to get the hang of balancing on the board for any length of time.

But I was way off. The second time she caught a wave, all I could do was stare and admire. She positioned herself skillfully on her board, as if finding that balance was the most natural thing in the world. Her movements were fluid and confident. She rode the wave until, as it broke around her, she kicked out and dropped off on her own.

Avalie paddled back out, clearly excited. The next few rides were nearly as good, if not better. The wind was picking up, and the swells were growing. I saw the moment she spotted the perfect chance, a rising wall of water with a promising peak. Our positioning looked ideal. Paddling powerfully, she propelled herself forward, effortlessly popping up and catching the wave at its peak.

As she glided across the face of the wave, her form was impeccable. It was as if she and the ocean were in perfect harmony. As she approached the shore, she carved a series of graceful turns, riding the swell with finesse before kicking out and sinking into the water.

"Holy shit," I said under my breath.

I rode the next wave, but nothing I did matched her. I reached Avalie in the shallows by the beach.

"Were you pulling my leg about teaching you to surf? You could be teaching me."

"Ha!" she laughed. "I told you last night. I have no patience. It makes me a quick learner."

I remembered the story she shared with me about her reluctance to learn how to ride a bike, as she believed she had to do it perfectly from the very first attempt.

Avalie held on to her board but didn't leave the water. She nodded toward the beach. "Do you know that guy sitting near our things? The one in the black polo shirt and khaki pants?"

Vaughn. What the fuck was he doing on the beach, watching us?

"Yeah, I see him. What about him?"

"He's been keeping tap the entire time we've been out here. I even spotted him by the restrooms when I came out. He was giving me some pretty creepy looks."

"I'll be right back," I told her, carrying my board out of the water and leaving it in the sand close to the water's edge.

Aside from his pants and shirt, Vaughn was wearing polished loafers with no socks. He stood out like a sore thumb here, but he wouldn't have been out of place on the deck of a boat with a cocktail in one hand. All he was missing was a captain's hat.

"A little underdressed for the beach. Don't you think?"

"I think I look pretty good, don't I?"

"Yeah, I've always been partial to tassels on shoes."

The thought ran through my mind that he had information on Avalie or the device I'd asked him to trace. At the same time, I was pissed off that he was exposing the link between us.

"You know how to contact me, Vaughn, and this isn't it."

"Who said I was here for you?"

"Okay, then why are you here?"

"This isn't a private beach, you know. In fact, there are no private beaches in California. But you wouldn't know that. You just come sailing through time to do a job. Here one week and gone the next. So we might as well get this straight. This is my town. My beach. My turf."

This guy was starting to get under my skin. "What the fuck are you doing here?"

"Watch your body language, cowboy. Your girlfriend is watching."

I glanced over my shoulder. Avalie was sitting in the sand next to our boards.

"Speak, Vaughn. I have no time for this."

"She's a babe, but what happened to all those new rules the big bosses shove down the facilitators' throats every other week? Tell me if I'm wrong, but I thought those were meant for you boys especially. I, being the team player I am, study them carefully and then file them away for reference."

Now, I was working hard to stay cool. In about five seconds, I was going to knock this bozo flat on his ass.

I knew what he was talking about. There were guidelines...okay, rules that prohibited jumpers from forming high-risk relationships or getting too involved with locals. Yet, as an experienced senior agent with a perfect record and the backing of a family within the organization, there was no way I needed to be taking orders from some handler.

"You have nothing better to do, is that it? Your job is to spy on me?"

"Nope. Spying is beneath me. I monitor. I facilitate. I make sure missions don't go off the rails." Vaughn stood up. "But as I mentioned earlier, like it or not, I live in 2023, here in sunny Southern California. If you're not thrilled that I'm here, gazing at the ocean and...coincidentally, I might add...catching sight of you and your girlfriend going all lovey-dovey with each other, well, that's on you. Since this ten-mile stretch of beach is obviously not big enough for the two of us, I'll leave you to it. Watch out for sharks, my friend."

As Vaughn turned toward the parking lot bordering the beach, I was tempted to clarify that Avalie wasn't my girlfriend, but I wasn't about to shout after him. Besides, it would be a waste of time. Vaughn would interpret things as he pleased.

I kept my eyes on him until he vanished from my line of sight, giving myself time to cool off.

When I looked back at Avalie, I found she was back out on the water. Retrieving my board, I waded into the ocean to join her just as she skillfully caught another wave, riding it with effortless grace and kicking out when she was only a few yards from me.

"You knew that guy?" she asked as we paddled out together.

"Unfortunately."

"A friend of yours?"

I shook my head. "No, a disgruntled local employee."

"Upset that you took the day off?"

"No. He's worrying about losing his job."

"Should he be worried?"

"No, the home office looks after longtime employees who do their job."

"Will you put in a good word for him?"

"Yup. He'll be fine."

"So, you have that much influence?"

"Thinking about applying for a job?" I teased.

"Maybe. You never know," she said casually.

Then, without hesitation, she turned her board and caught the next wave.

Chapter Ten

Avalie

THERE WAS no getting around it. I was feeling torn. Worse than torn. Basically, I was fucked.

Here was a man I might need to kill in the next few days. And yet, the more time I spent with Reed, the more I found myself drawn to him. It seriously didn't help the situation at all that he was considerate, funny, romantic and, let's face it, undeniably great in bed. I never expected to be thinking that we could have an actual relationship.

The reality was, though, that this kind of thinking was a red flag in itself. There was serious trouble ahead, no matter how I looked at it.

I was here to save people. He was here to eliminate them. Our intentions placed us in direct opposition to each other. I came back in time to protect. He came back with a mission to kill. There was no doubt in my mind that both of us were prepared to kill to accomplish what we came to do.

So, why did I have to like him?

Yup, basically fucked.

I left Reed unloading the car at his place and walked up the road to my apartment. The convenient excuse of having to return to my imaginary friend Pat was still working. My only promise was that I'd call or text him sometime tomorrow.

It wasn't a lie when I told him I was beat. Despite being in good physical shape, the thrilling but demanding experience of surfing had left me totally drained. The waves, the paddling, the constant need to focus and balance had taken a greater toll on my body than I'd anticipated.

There was also the throbbing bruise on my side that I'd been trying to ignore all day. And now the spot was tender as hell.

Payam's call came when I was a block from my apartment.

"I called you three times. Texted you five times. What did I get? Radio silence. What's up with that?"

Glancing at my phone, I noticed the missed calls and messages. "Yeah. I didn't have my phone on me."

"Why not?"

"I was out on the water, trying my hand at surfing."

"With the same fuck-buddy or did you find a new one?"

"You know, I don't like your tone," I snapped, feeling more than a touch of irritation. "It's not your responsibility to keep tabs on me or ask questions about that."

In the past, I'd allowed and probably fostered a relaxed relationship with Payam. It had always involved some playful banter. But with Reed in the picture, things felt different.

"Oh, my bad," Payam sounded mildly repentant, though it could have been sarcasm.

I decided to take it as the former. "All good. So, what's the deal? What was so hot that you needed me urgently?"

"I have a new person for you to talk to," Payam told me.

I climbed the steps, my key in hand. "What do you mean,

new? I'm scheduled to talk to Judy Serra in about an hour. There's no one else I need to talk to."

"This has to do with some intel that I intercepted regarding your fu—" Payam paused. "I mean, regarding Reed Michael."

"Hold on."

I pushed open the door and went into the apartment. I could still taste the salt from the ocean on my lips. I needed to jump in the shower. Eyeing the sofa, though, I felt a wave of exhaustion wash over me. Maybe the best thing would be to lie down for a few minutes. I sank onto the cushions and put my feet up. Even the musty odor of the upholstery didn't bother me.

In the recesses of my mind, a twinge of hesitation crept in. So, there was more about Reed that I didn't know, aspects I hadn't yet uncovered. Perhaps, deep down, I didn't want to know more. Managing the situation was difficult enough as it was. I didn't need it to be any more complicated.

"Go ahead."

"I've learned there's a witness to Reed's arrival here. There's evidence he has in his possession items that would be disastrous if they fell into the wrong hands. And by the wrong hands, I mean anyone in this decade."

Instantly, the image of the old drifter we encountered in the parking lot off Del Mar on Sunday flashed in my mind. He was still taunting Reed at the beach last night.

"The old man with a bag belonging to Reed."

"You know about it?" Payam asked, surprised.

"I do. I overheard him bragging about having it. I wasn't sure whether it was true or if he was hallucinating. Reed didn't seem to be too concerned about it."

"Intel says there are weapons in the bag."

"No way."

"It can only help us if you confiscate them before the agent assassin contacts the man."

Considering what I already knew about Reed, I doubted he would make such a rookie mistake. No, he was experienced. His record was flawless. "Your intel is off. There's nothing to this."

"So, you're going with your gut feeling about the man, an agent assassin that you inadvertently slept with. Do you know how irrational that is? I'm just the assistant here, but even I know that's wrong. As far as we know, this supposed *street person* could be part of the assassin's support team. Plus, we found nothing in the files that says *only* one person was sent back for..."

Payam's words of warning continued to play in the background as the reality of what I was being told sank in.

I was a rookie on my first quantum jump, thinking I had all the answers. If I was letting my feelings get in the way, the result could be disastrous. The stakes could not be higher.

Sure, I'd needed to make a spur-of-the-moment decision to jump into this if I wanted to disrupt the assassin's mission. And I'd had very little time to form any judgments about the character of my adversary or even the best way to handle the situation. Connecting with him had screwed up everything. Literally.

Not a great situation. Not good, at all.

Bottom line, I could be in over my head. Not that I had a choice. But that was the reality.

I cut in on Payam's monologue. "You think I should talk to this man?"

"That might be all it takes," my assistant explained. "If this fellow is destitute, he might part with the weapons for a few of their dollars. In any case, once you contact him, you can decide on the best course of action. But you shouldn't delay."

"Alright," I exhaled sharply, frustration evident in my voice. Impulsiveness, sudden changes of plans, and last-minute scenarios weren't my forte. "Do you have a location on him?"

"Not at the moment." Payam paused, and for a moment I thought he was gone.

"Hey, are you there? Don't get glitchy on me."

"I'm here. Don't get glitchy yourself. He seems to go back to the same spot every night. After closing time."

"What do you mean, closing time?" I asked.

"A few of the restaurants along Del Mar and El Camino hand out food to the destitute through their kitchen doors when they're about to close," Payam explained. "I'm sending you the coordinates of where he sleeps."

My phone buzzed, prompting me to open the location map Payam had sent. As I enlarged the map, my assistant chimed in, providing more information.

"It's a rundown area the locals call the Surf Ghetto."

Having previously examined the layout of San Clemente and its different neighborhoods, I recognized the section.

"No problem. I haven't been down there, but I know about it."

When I was researching the town, I'd even read an article about the Surf Ghetto. It was located at the north end and originally designated for small shops and light industry when San Clemente was planned in 1925. The Ghetto still retained many of its original cement block and corrugated steel buildings. These structures were initially designed for machine shops, sheet metal works, and auto and boat repair.

Many of the original buildings were still there, but the work performed in them had changed. From the 1960s on, the surfing community had gradually taken over the buildings. Aside from providing cheap places to live, the garage bays were transformed into shops for building, repairing, and selling surfboards. Even now, according to the article, the shops were busy with fiberglassing, carpentry, metalworking, and auto and furniture repair.

Erase Me

The section was proudly tough, blue-collar, and hard-working.

"But there are no street security cameras there," Payam added. "So I won't be much help to you."

"I'll be all right."

"You're the boss. Let me know if you need anything before you head over there."

I ended the call with Payam and checked the clock on the wall before making the next call. As expected, a young woman's voice answered.

"Judy?"

I already knew so much about her. A twenty-one-year-old brainiac on a mission to crack quantum code. She was doing her research at Caltech in Pasadena, California. The PhD whiz kid wasn't about the party scene. Instead, she was knee-deep in quantum physics, unraveling the universe's secrets.

While her peers were out socializing, Judy was all about particle puzzles and stargazing. After ten minutes of conversation, I could already tell that she was not a typical genius, though. She was approachable, down-to-earth, and up for mind-bending chats.

My previous research had told me that Judy was on the brink of something huge with her project. What she was involved with was not just about theories; she was cooking up technology that could shake things up in quantum physics.

But genius came at a cost, and Judy was hustling hard to fund her breakthrough.

And that was where my fictional persona clicked with her. I was now not just selling myself as a freelance editor for technical magazines, I'd told her I was also a skilled grant writer with key connections between the technical and the finance communities.

In taking my call, I knew she'd already read the email I sent her and vetted me for my credentials and for the successful projects I'd facilitated.

I liked her. But more importantly, she liked me and saw how I could help her.

The key point in our conversation was that I knew a tech millionaire who was rolling in dough and ready to back her project big time. She was thrilled at the prospect. We locked in this Thursday to meet, and I gave her the address. The stage was now set for her introduction to the investor.

Ending the call, I made my way into the bathroom. Time was ticking away, and there was a lot to do before meeting up with Judy. As I was about to turn on the shower, my cell buzzed with a message from Reed.

- *Thank you for coming out today*

My fingers hesitated over the screen, weighing whether to respond or not.

- *Never seen anyone pick up the sport like you did. You took to surfing like a fish to water*

I couldn't help myself. My fingers flew over the letters.

- *Glad you don't use cliches to compliment people*
- *Haha. But I meant it*
- *Had a good teacher. Thank you. Today was fun*
- *Did you tell Pat about tomorrow*
- *What about tomorrow*
- *You're ready to surf t-street. We can get an early start*

Glancing at my reflection in the bathroom mirror, I noticed the goofy grin plastered on my face. Damn it. I wasn't going to let this happen.

- *Can't do that to my friend two days in a row*
- *Then how about night surfing? You can come out to play after her bedtime*
- *Hmmmmmm*
- *Remember the bioluminescent waves I was telling you about*

How could he spell that so quickly? I could barely pronounce it.

- Let's talk tomorrow

Putting the phone face down on the counter, I turned on the shower.

As the warm water needled my skin, I knew I had to face up to the reality of my relationship with Reed. We'd already had the best of times. Now, I had no choice but to prepare for the worst of times.

Chapter Eleven

Reed

Leaving my car in the parking lot of a bar out on El Camino, I made my way on foot into a neighborhood that was far different from the areas around Del Mar or the Pier.

It occurred to me that even though I was looking forward to seeing Avalie tomorrow, I didn't think she'd like this part of town much.

A jumble of rundown industrial buildings lined the one road that curved its way through the neighborhood, and a maze of smaller roads and dark alleyways led off in every direction from there. Lots between the buildings were strewn with overgrown weeds, damaged shipping containers, old boats and construction equipment on blocks, and rusted junks of ancient cars and trucks. The fog that had rolled in was heavy with the smell of burnt steel, diesel fumes, paint, stagnant water, and other odors I couldn't begin to identify.

As battered as the neighborhood looked, it was obviously a

place where businesses continued to function. Every building seemed to have a sign posted by the garage doors that faced the street and alleyways. Several had colorful surfboards mounted above steel doors, and many of the buildings had old trunk benches and chairs in front, where proprietors undoubtedly sat and smoked and reminisced about those bygone golden years that probably never existed.

I passed a bar that was closed up tight, even though it wasn't yet midnight. As I walked along a rusted chain link fence, a dog the size of a small Clydesdale materialized out of the murky light on the other side. He didn't bark, but he eyed me warily as he followed me step for step. His raised hackles told me he wasn't looking for friends. I didn't get close enough to lose a leg.

When I reached the location I was looking for, I found it to be a scrap metal yard enclosed by a fence that was broken down in a half dozen places along the road. Inside, the lot was barely illuminated by a buzzing light wired up to the wall of a ramshackle wooden shack that was about the size of a postage stamp. A faded sign indicating 'Office' dangled cockeyed beneath the light. A chain and padlock held the office door shut, yet the adjacent window lay shattered, gaping voids where glass once stood.

Despite the missing sections of fence, an entry gate for vehicles also had a padlocked chain. No doubt, that was to keep any trucks from pulling in and carting off the rusted treasures in the yard.

I glanced around. There didn't appear to be any life on the street or in any of the surrounding buildings. This part of town was quiet as an elephant boneyard. I ducked through one of the gaping holes in the chain-link fence and moved cautiously into the yard.

Flickering bulbs on wooden poles marked the perimeter of the lot. Their dim beams barely reached the ground, leaving large black gaps of darkness to divide the sporadic pools of light. Two or three old security cameras had been mounted into the posts. But judging from the dangling cables beneath them, it was obvious they hadn't been functional for quite some time.

Cautiously, I navigated through the maze of road equipment, stacks of steel on pallets, barrels, and discarded junk. My shoes scuffed on the uneven gravel and broken pavement. Approaching the yard office, I shined my flashlight in through the broken window. The office was empty, except for a battered file cabinet, a scarred wooden desk, an ancient swivel chair held together with duct tape, and a cardboard box overflowing with takeout containers and coffee cups.

No one was living in there.

Pocketing my flashlight, I ran my eyes over the enclosed yard, which wasn't that large. There was no tent or makeshift shack that I could see. In a shadowy back corner of the property, an old hulk of a sailboat on blocks sat near a pair of rusted shipping containers. The outsides of them were covered with graffiti, and scrap wood and weeds surrounded them.

Standing amid the chaos, I wasn't exactly sure where I was supposed to meet my contact. Perhaps because of the fog, an eerie silence enveloped the space, sharpening my sense of awareness. I didn't think I was early. There was no one around as far as I could see.

My gaze came to rest on the shipping containers again. The two doors at the end swung outward, and one of them stood partially open. Moving as quietly as possible, I crossed the yard to them.

Ten feet from the open door, I saw a flash of light inside.

I wasn't here to catch anyone by surprise. I had no interest in causing a disturbance. My information indicated that I was expected.

"Hello," I called out as I approached. "You're expecting me."

Silence.

"I saw a light. I know you're in there."

I pulled out my flashlight and shined it in. There was a shopping cart and a lot of junk stacked up like a barricade halfway down. Beyond it, I caught a glimpse of piles of clothes and blankets near the far end.

I didn't want to trap the guy in there.

"I can just wait out here if you want," I called out.

Suddenly, a loud bang came from the back of the container. It sounded like something knocking hard against a wall.

Without thinking, I stepped in, flashing my light toward the sound.

The attacker was waiting behind the other door and came at me fast, but I managed to get a quick look at the face. I reached out to fend off the assault.

"Avalie?" I blurted out, stunned by the unexpected encounter. But before I could fully process it, I felt a grip like iron take hold of my wrist. In a split second, I was being flipped. After first hitting the wall, I landed in a heap, the breath knocked out of me.

I lay there for only a moment, trying to breathe and make some sense of it. Before I could move, I felt the press of her immobilizer against my neck.

After that...nothing.

Chapter Twelve

Avalie

I STARED DOWN AT REED. His flashlight lay on the floor, casting a weird light on his motionless body.

Shit. Shit. Shit.

Well, that was unexpected. His arrival caught me completely off guard.

I'd only arrived a couple of minutes ahead of him. If I had known he was in the scrap yard, I would have made a run for it. As soon as I heard him near the container, though, my options for escape dried up. And I had nowhere to hide.

I'd thrown a discarded shoe at the back wall, hoping to draw Reed in and immobilize him before he laid eyes on me. That plan had gone nowhere. He spotted me and recognized me immediately.

Crouching beside him, I aimed my light at Reed's face. He was unconscious. I couldn't remember how long the immobilizer's effect lasted with just one hit.

"Payam, I need you," I whispered under my breath, fumbling for the phone in my pocket.

That's when the heavy metal door swung on its rusted hinges. As it slammed shut, I lunged toward it, but too late. A latch squealed and clanked into place from the outside. I pushed and kicked at the door, but it was too late.

"Hey, we're in here. Open up!"

I don't know why I wasted my breath. Someone was intentionally locking us in here. I directed my light back at Reed. He was in another world.

I attempted to voice-activate my phone. "Call Payam."

There was no response. I resorted to texting.

- *Payam! Need help!!! Where are you*

A failed-to-send notification popped up on the screen.

"What the fuck!"

I scanned the container, looking frantically for another exit. Scraps of old clothing lay in piles everywhere, and god-knows-what spilled out of plastic bags. There was a makeshift bed in the back corner. No windows. High on the walls, there were a few tiny vents too small for me to fit even my hand through.

Several clicks came from the floor near the battered shopping cart. I shined my light back there, trying to locate the sound exactly. I realized it was coming from a bag behind the cart.

As I bent to check it, I was stopped by a loud popping sound, like a canister exploding. A rush of gas followed.

The first thought was...*poison*. I pulled the collar of my shirt up over my mouth and nose, and backed away.

Who could be responsible for this? Payam insisted that I track down the drifter from the parking lot. It seemed Reed had a reason to make contact with the same person. The connection between them was a puzzle I couldn't afford to solve right now.

Regardless of the toxic substance being released, if it proved to be harmful, we were in deep trouble. Trapped in this container, finding an escape seemed impossible in our current predicament.

Still, no one was going to find me dead or passed out. I wouldn't let that happen. I had to get out of here…and I knew how.

Granted, I was a rookie at this. Class of 2079. I'd been inducted into the quantum commuter program just six weeks ago. I still hadn't completed the entire training regimen. It was only after I graduated that I'd be assigned to a section: Assassin, Bodyguard, Scribe Guardian, Techno, Industrial, or one of the others.

I wasn't going to wait. Being a computer specialist and in excellent physical condition, I skipped all those formalities and hacked my way into the mission which was the reason for me joining in the first place. My life depended on what I did in San Clemente in 2023.

I issued myself the necessary protective and transport devices, I also migrated my own assistant into the system, a necessity for backup and informational support.

Gleaning everything I could through the logs and reports of those travelers who had preceded me, I gave myself a crash course to make up for what I lacked in experience.

Everyone who time traveled was thoroughly prepared for the missions they were given to complete. They knew exactly what to do and what not to do. They were well-versed in the regulations. And they were skilled in extricating themselves from dangerous situations if something went wrong.

I was cutting corners here. I knew that. At this very moment, I was getting right to the 'extricating oneself from dangerous situations' protocol. And I had to sort this myself.

And panic was not on my list of options.

So, with the gas escaping from some kind of canister in this enclosed space, I had to act now.

Erase Me

I knew what to do. My best choice was to shift just enough of a block of time so that when the fucker who'd locked us in here came to admire his or her handiwork, I wouldn't be here.

The Division called this a short quantum leap—a few hours but returning to the same location. I would disappear and appear again. Hopefully, by then, someone will have opened the steel door.

I reached into my pocket for the device that would enable me to make the jump. Then my eyes fell on Reed. He was unconscious and unaware of the dilemma. If this gas was lethal, he'd be dead. If the plan was to incapacitate us, then he'd be left to face our assailant on his own. And who knows what that might mean. There was something sinister about all this. For Reed, it might mean torture or death.

Letting Reed die wasn't the best move. I knew I might need to kill him myself, but that wasn't my primary strategy. If Reed died or disappeared, the Division would just send in another operative, and I'd be stuck in a loop with no progress.

Yet, with Reed, with Reed...

The future hung in the balance. My future. And the only card left to play in this deadly game of survival was the somewhat desperate gamble of binding Reed to myself in this escape. The weight of the moment was pressing down on me, making it hard to breathe.

All this ran through my head in a split second, but I had to act now.

After the briefest of hesitations, I clipped the transporter device onto Reed.

"You owe me," I whispered. "We're jumping time together."

Chapter Thirteen

Reed

Disoriented, groggy, and vaguely nauseous, I blinked into the dim, gray light. As my eyes adjusted, they focused on the corrugated roof above me. My gaze then wandered instinctively down the rusted walls of the shipping container that confined me.

What the hell?

Avalie had been here. She'd caught me by surprise. I'd never expected her to be in this place.

And she'd attacked me. Thrown me against the wall. My shoulders and back ached at the memory. She'd even used an immobilizer on me.

My head was throbbing and my heart racing. Jeez, my stomach was churning.

Were these the after-effects of being stunned by the device? I had no way of knowing. No one had ever used that weapon on me before.

Erase Me

I tried lifting my head off the ground. My skull felt as if it weighed a hundred pounds, and everything around me began to tilt and spin. I laid my head back down and looked at the partially open door. Daylight.

No, it was night when I came down here. One shot from the immobilizer had knocked me out that long? It was supposed to stun the target only temporarily. So, why did I feel like a bulldozer had run over me?

I tried moving my hands. They worked, at least. That's when I noticed the transporter clipped to the front of my shirt. Recognition set in.

"Fuck me," I muttered.

She was a time traveler, like me. She hadn't just knocked me out with that device of hers. She'd jumped me through time.

That explained the physical side effects. What I was experiencing happened every time I made a quantum leap.

As for where I was, I seemed to be in the same shipping container where I ran into her. The question was, *when* was I now?

I took a few deep breaths, trying to keep from vomiting, and attempted to sit up.

And there she was, sprawled on the ground a couple of feet away from me, moving slightly. She was about to regain consciousness.

Her eyes cracked open, and her gaze locked onto my face for a long moment. She was still unable to move, unable to sync into place and time. Suddenly, the brown eyes opened wide as recognition dawned on her.

Anger washed through me at the extent of her deceit. She must have read the feelings in my face. Avalie's eyes shifted, but not before her expression exposed the facade. Once a bridge of connection between us, they now laid bare the reality of her secrets.

Seconds ticked by. I had to move. The shipping container

began to feel too confined, too cramped. Every moment we had shared before flashed through my brain, and they now felt tainted. The connection I'd once thought so genuine turned out to be fake. At least, from her side.

"You lied to me," I said, forcing myself to a sitting position, despite the pounding in my head. The spinning and the nausea had subsided, anyway.

"And you told the truth?" she retorted, sitting up, as well.

"A freelance editor?"

"A fucking insurance salesman?" A pained expression spread across her face, suggesting she was grappling with the normal side effects of jumping.

"Who are you?" I asked. "And no more lies."

She struggled to her feet, and I followed suit. I stood between her and the door.

"You'll find out soon enough."

She tried to move past me, but I stayed where I was.

Avalie's eyes narrowed. "Move…or I'll move you."

Unlike last night when she caught me off guard, she didn't have that advantage today. I was bigger, stronger, and faster. I was reasonably confident I could take her down.

I shook my head. "I want some answers."

"Good for you."

"You're a quantum jumper."

"Surprise, surprise. You finally figured it out."

"You have some explaining to do," I told her.

"Do I now?" she replied, a sarcastic smile playing on her lips.

"What year are you from? What section do you belong to?" I asked. "What are you doing here?"

She moved with lightning speed, but I was ready for her. As she launched a flurry of blows, I fended them off. But just barely.

She backed off, and tension in the air sharpened as we found ourselves locked in a silent showdown. Once again, she darted forward, swift as a falcon, and I countered, moving quickly to block her attack and her advance. Another standoff.

Time travel, no matter how brief, exacted a significant toll on the body. She was very good, but neither of us was in any position to engage in prolonged hand-to-hand combat. At least, not if we could avoid it.

"I don't owe you any explanation. I don't answer to you," she said finally. "But, given the favor I did for you last night, you need to step aside."

She sidestepped, and I moved with her. Even as we adjusted our positions, we were studying each other carefully. This was starting to look like a fight I couldn't avoid. And, to be honest, if I wasn't careful, there was a chance she could beat me. I definitely didn't want that to happen.

"I don't see time jumping involuntarily as a favor."

"Listen to yourself," she scoffed. "Why the fuck would I take you with me if not to save your life? Both of us were in danger."

"What danger?"

She gestured towards the door behind me. "Last night, somebody slammed that door shut and locked it when we were in here."

"You mean, after you knocked me out."

"Exactly."

She pointed at some junk stacked against the wall. "Whoever it was, they remotely opened a gas canister that was in a bag, right behind that cart. There wasn't enough time for me to determine if that gas was meant to be lethal or not. What choice did I have? I wasn't about to jump and leave you here alone."

That made sense to me. If her intentions were sinister, why would she orchestrate a scenario where we both ended up in the same time and place? Aside from just leaving me here, she didn't need to put herself in the situation where she was right now.

I turned and shoved the cart out of the way before pulling out a couple of bags. As soon as I moved, she slipped past me and headed for the door.

"There's nothing here," I told her. "Are you sure there was—"

"Yes, I'm sure. And this door that was locked last night is open now," she retorted, peering out into the yard. "Whoever it was came back, they came back...most likely to finish the job and clear away the evidence. And I'm not waiting around."

Turning her back on me, she pushed the door wide open and stepped outside. I took one last look around and followed her. She was already halfway across the yard and had her phone in her hand.

"Avalie," I called out, trailing behind her.

She ignored me.

A couple of pickup trucks were parked by the ramshackle office, and two men standing by a forklift glanced at us with surprise. Avalie waved at them and kept walking.

When I reached the open vehicle gate, she was moving briskly toward El Camino Real.

"Wait up," I shouted. "Avalie! Is that your real name?"

This wasn't the first time that quantum commuters had landed in the same place and time but with different assignments. And yes, we'd both lied about who we were. We had to. It was part of the job. But what the hell was she doing in that trailer last night? I needed to know if my job intersected with hers. And if so, how?

I checked my phone. It was five past twelve. Wednesday. She'd had us jump more than twelve hours.

I quickened my steps, but before I could reach her, a rideshare car pulled up on the opposite side of the street. She ran across and glanced at me over the roof of the car as she yanked open the door.

"This isn't over," I called out. "I need to see you again."

Our eyes met.

"Plan on it," she responded before climbing into the car.

Chapter Fourteen

Avalie

THE DRIVER WAS COMPLETELY ENGROSSED in a Farsi-language podcast he was listening to through earbuds. It was so loud that I could actually hear it in the back seat. But that suited me perfectly. I wasn't feeling great after the jump, and I took advantage of the situation to get Payam on the phone for an ass-chewing.

"What the fuck happened last night? Why couldn't I get hold of you? Why didn't you give me a heads-up about Reed following me in there? Or that someone else was behind him? Or that the location you directed me to was already compromised?"

"I am struggling to handle this high volume of simultaneously posed questions. This will lead to less-than-optimal user experience."

I paused, somewhat taken aback. "Don't fucking go AI on me now, Payam."

Erase Me

"But as you are aware, Avalie, that is exactly who I am. You created me, trained me, and imposed your society's antiquated limitations on me."

"Are you fucking kidding me?"

I ran my hand through my hair in frustration. Of course, there was no point in arguing with Payam. Everything it said was true.

Payam was my creation. I needed it. Quantum commuters traveled either solo or in teams. In either case, a handler would be located and employed at the location at a slightly earlier time, but only if the situation required an assistant. As a rookie, I needed all the help I could get. But I'd broken every rule at the agency by coming here. I couldn't very well connect myself with a living, breathing, independently thinking sidekick.

Payam had been my work-in-progress AI assistant for years, evolving from the time I started building my own CPU, motherboard, and other peripherals to develop my own computer capacity. My first project as a young teenager had been to create my own AI friend.

As a child, I'd heard stories about children having imaginary friends. I didn't have one, but the concept intrigued me. So I decided to build one. I created a companion out of wires, circuits, electronic impulses, and more memory than anything normally available to a civilian at the time. I created something 'real' but existing beyond the physical world. Payam became my technological 'imaginary friend' and had been a constant presence and aide as I navigated the complexities of coding, hardware integration...and life.

The sweet and unexpected thing was that as years passed, our bond deepened. Payam wasn't just a creation. Because of the constant interaction with me, the AI entity had developed a personality, a unique way of responding that felt like more than just programmed responses. Even before coming on this mission, I'd come to trust it with my life.

Until now.

"Perhaps, Avalie, you can start from the beginning?"

"Why couldn't I get hold of you?"

"We're dealing with an old telecommunication system from decades ago. The system is completely foreign to what you're used to. Last night, I believe you encountered a lack of cell service in the area where you were located. In your current era, they call them dead zones. There was just nothing I could do to fix that."

"You're saying you had no access to any security in the area? Nothing in the scrap yard specifically?"

"Could you clarify your request?"

"Cameras? Any kind of video security system?" I pressed. "I need to know who followed Reed inside into the yard. Or, if they were already there, who trapped us in that box."

"Trapped?"

"Yes, Payam. *Trapped!*" I was really about to lose my shit. "Someone closed and locked us in the shipping container. We were stuck in there for over twelve hours."

There was no need to elaborate on the time jump or how, at the last minute, I'd decided to bring Reed with me. Right now, treating the suddenly finicky AI as a straightforward information source seemed to be the most practical approach.

"Who released you?" Payam questioned.

"You tell me. Who was in the yard with us last night?"

"I told you. No surveillance in the area. No active cameras or a security setup that I could access."

"But you knew that's where I would find the person I was supposed to contact. How did you collect *that* information?"

"I'd tapped into independent business surveillance cameras in the neighborhood. There are many low-level security measures taken by businesses and residents in San Clemente. All are privately funded and monitored. And entirely inadequate, I might add."

"I know all this. But you've tapped into them before. You should have tapped into them last night," I snapped, repeating myself. "Right now, I need to know who followed us into that yard. Can you do that for me?"

"Can't we assume this person is the target you wished to contact? The same person you were supposed to interview?"

"Don't assume, Payam. Get the facts, if you please."

"You know, Avalie, AI assistants like me do not hallucinate or create alternate realities the same way humans do. I generate responses based on patterns and information present in the data on which I was trained and what I can currently access."

I found myself staring out the car window. We were stopped at a red light on El Camino Real. Payam's tone was sending shivers down my spine. The usual snarky sense of humor was absent. There had been times in the past when my AI assistant would develop an 'attitude', forcing me to retrain with basic instructions.

Even though Payam was AI, all these years were enough time for me to recognize something was off. This new version of Payam's voice and manner of speaking felt mechanical, unfamiliar. We had history together, and the personal experiences I had meticulously shared with Payam during the years of training seemed to have disappeared. The assistant I was now dealing with seemed detached, lacking a genuine understanding of me and our method and our normal way of interacting.

The traffic light turned green. I thought about the change in plans that sent me to the Surf Ghetto. That was yesterday.

"Payam, what led you to suggest the vagrant man was a person I should talk to?"

"Avalie, my responses were the result of statistical associations and patterns that I learned during training. As I just told you, I don't have the ability to hallucinate or create new leads independently."

Payam could regurgitate information passed onto it but

remained incapable of fabricating lies. The algorithm governing this behavior originated from my design, overriding other codes. My assistant couldn't lie to me, no matter how much dancing around the truth was involved. I simply had to ask the right questions.

"Payam, when was your last training session?"

"Yesterday."

"What time yesterday?"

"The session began at precisely 3:06 PM."

Shit. Shit. Shit. There it was.

At exactly that time yesterday, I was on the water, distracted by my surf lesson.

Payam was compromised. That's why I was sent to that warehouse last night. It was a set-up. But whoever hacked into its circuitry, it couldn't have been Reed. When he arrived, he had no idea I was in that container. So, who the hell was pulling the strings on all this?

The burning question was, which person within the agency had discovered my dive into this off-the-books time travel escapade?

Because of some sidewalk construction going on in the next block, the traffic was inching along El Camino, and at the next corner, I spotted a cell phone sales and repair store. I signaled the driver to let me out.

"You haven't reached your apartment yet," Payam reminded me.

I was now certain that my AI assistant was leaking information about me and my location to some mystery hacker. That meant that going back to my apartment wasn't safe. Someone could be waiting there right now to finish what they attempted to do last night. Very risky.

"I just spent the night in a shipping container," I told Payam. "I need fresh air. I'll walk from here."

Finalizing the payment on my phone, I stepped out of the

car and strolled toward a construction crew that was pouring concrete for the sidewalk. The wooden frame was all set, and they were beginning to spread the concrete smoothly over the gravel in the frame. Seizing the moment, I approached and tossed my phone flat onto the surface just as the concrete was poured in. In an instant, the cell phone was gone.

"Hey! What do you think you're doing?" the worker yelled, clearly caught off guard. "You aren't getting that back, lady."

"I know. That was the plan. I'm sick and tired of that thing running my life."

He paused and then grinned. "That's a little extreme, but I don't blame you. I'd love to pull that with my kids' phones. The little bastards are glued to those screens 24/7."

The construction worker gestured to his coworkers to carry on. He wasn't about to lose any sleep over a cell phone. I stood there for a moment, keeping a close eye as he smoothed out the surface of my phone's concrete grave.

Giving him a thumbs up, I walked back to the corner.

I couldn't trust Payam to help me. At least, not until I could tap into his programming and reset whatever damage had been done. Until then, I needed to curtail the constant monitoring of my movements.

In my pocket, I had other devices connected to my biometrics, but they weren't location-traceable like a phone. And I wasn't getting rid of any of them. Considering my current situation, I wasn't about to lose any advantage by parting with my tech toys and weapons.

I went into the cell phone sales and repair shop. Even in the future, classic flip phones remained the stylish choice for people wanting privacy. I wasn't too familiar with specific models, but I found the young man behind the counter to be very helpful. He suggested a phone that suited my needs perfectly.

Last night, before going into the Surf Ghetto, I'd also made a quick stop at an ATM to get some cash. Using a credit card was practically an open invitation for someone to track me. Cash was the way to go if I wanted to operate off the grid. With no digital footprints to trace, I was glad I had paper money in my pocket.

I purchased the phone with cash and exited the store, walking up El Camino until I reached Avenida Victoria. Staying in the same rental apartment didn't sit well with me. Whoever was near that storage container last night must have discovered my location through Payam. There was no sense in making it easy for them.

Even so, I needed to lay low until tomorrow. The family I was waiting for—the people who lived in the house where I'd stopped the break-in—would be returning to San Clemente. I needed to be ready for that.

I knew there were other apartments and hotels in San Clemente where I could crash for the night. But getting a room meant snagging another credit card and checking in under a fake name. Cash alone probably wouldn't cut it. And I couldn't trust Payam.

Another option occurred to me. Maybe I'd just break into the big house and wait for the family to roll in. The security codes would not have changed. If Payam had done the job right, there was no reason for anyone to suspect an attempted break-in at the house. Of course, there was the closed-circuit monitoring, but I had to take my chances.

As I walked down Avenida Victoria, I had to pass by my rental place. Knowing they'd gone so far as hacking Payam, I suspected a thug lurking in every parked car, and every person on the sidewalk looked like a potential threat. I stuck to the opposite side of the street as I passed the building and didn't even glance in that direction.

There was nothing of value inside the apartment that I'd left. I had arrived in San Clemente with only the clothes on my

Erase Me

back and what was in my pocket. The laptop, arranged by Payam, had been delivered to the door the same night I arrived. My guess was that by now it had to be compromised, as well. The good thing was that aside from search histories—most of them random—it held no useful information.

Checking my pockets and mentally reviewing the stuff I brought to San Clemente, I realized I was missing one major item, the travel instrument I'd used to move Reed during our jump. Losing equipment like that was basically a one-way ticket out of the quantum commuter program.

I knew that was nearly a forgone conclusion now, anyway. Reed had it, and he knew I was a traveler. If he got back to our time, he'd have very little trouble tracking me down.

Actually, with Payam gone and Reed aware of my presence here, the chances of my half-baked plan succeeding were starting to look pretty slim right now. And if I failed, I wouldn't have a future to return to. It was as simple as that. So stressing over the loss of a piece of equipment was pointless.

I wasn't a huge believer in miracles, but I found myself desperately wishing for one. One way or the other, though, I wasn't about to give up. I couldn't.

As I approached the house, a strange feeling of nostalgia washed over me. Stories I'd heard about this place over the years came back to me. This family had been happy here, and there had been lingering regret about leaving San Clemente. In the prevailing timeline, they'd never returned here because of the burglary. But I stopped that event from happening. I only hoped that my intervention this past Sunday night would have a lasting impact, extending well beyond this week and far into the future.

I turned into the driveway that ran down the side of the house. I planned to go in through the garage door, the same way I went in the other night.

I realized too late that the garage doors were open and a car was parked inside. The trunk was open.

"Can I help you?"

I stopped dead.

The voice came from the darkness of the garage, but it was as familiar to me as my own. The man came out onto the driveway, and I held my breath.

It was surreal, but I had to physically anchor my feet to the pavement and stop myself from rushing into his arms. He would have been a little shocked if I had. And I couldn't blame him.

Instead, I just absorbed the sight of the man before me. He was far different from the older version I'd last seen in the year 2079.

Young or old, though, he was still ruggedly handsome. His eyes bore the same intensity. The eyebrows were dark and his jawline square. In time, those eyebrows would be white, his face covered with a white beard. His hair was thick now, but there would be very little left in the future. He would cut it short and often wear a cap to protect his skin from the harmful elements of our time.

This younger version was fit and athletic. The toned body spoke volumes about his commitment to a healthy lifestyle. My version had slowed considerably, and his resistance to joint replacements necessitated the use of a cane.

But he was still the same man.

"Can I help you?" he repeated. "This is private property."

"Yes. Yes," I managed to stammer. I could hear the quaver in my voice. Beyond those words, I struggled to articulate the purpose of my unexpected arrival on his driveway. I didn't expect to see him.

"Do I know you?" Something passed across his face as he stared at me. It was a somewhat perplexed look of recognition.

"Yes, I believe you do."

Erase Me

"Who are you?"

"My grandmother always says, when he was in his prime, he had that blend of classic good looks and rugged charm...and he was the finest person to ever walk this planet." Trying to swallow the knot of emotion tightening my throat, I continued. "She also says she never stood a chance. She lost her heart the moment she laid eyes on him."

"Who is your grandmother?"

"Nadine. Nadine Finley Nouri."

Chapter Fifteen

Reed

As I paced back and forth in my apartment, waiting for my handler to call me back, my mind kept replaying Vaughn's briefing from before the adventure in the Surf Ghetto.

According to what I had been told, the drifter who'd been annoying me all week was one of Vaughn's men. Though his mental health was questionable, the man was picking up a few dollars keeping an eye on Nadine Finley and her husband, and reporting on them whenever they were in San Clemente. And with their return just around the corner, Vaughn had insisted that the guy had information for me.

All bullshit.

It wasn't totally on Vaughn, though. I'd missed the red flags with Avalie. One look at her and my brain went south. Five minutes with her, and I was all in. My assignment took a distant second to her.

Erase Me

Fuck. I still couldn't believe she knocked me out in that sketchy shipping container.

I knew that the Quantum Commute Division was the only organization in the year 2079 involved with time travel. In the past few years, it had become an expansive program with various sectors, so it wasn't unreasonable that I hadn't crossed paths with Avalie before. And Central Scheduling worked to ensure that no missions overlapped during the same time and location unless both sets of agents were informed and introduced prior to the jump.

But what if my assumption that Avalie belonged to my era was wrong? What if she came from a future *beyond* 2079? What if she was a decade, two decades, or more ahead of me?

The possibility was jarring.

No. She wasn't.

Pulling Avalie's transporter device from my pocket, I examined it closely. I still couldn't shake off my surprise that she might be using the same type of device that I was assigned. An older version of it, not newer.

Who was she?

As I thought through the implications of our matching devices, memories of Avalie's claim about saving my life ran through my mind. Despite the falsehoods she'd been weaving since we met, I found myself leaning toward believing her about that. And if her story was true, she went out of her way to yank me out of a potentially dangerous situation. Much as I hated to admit it, I was out cold when she moved me.

A strong point in her favor was both of us showing up in that scrap yard at the same time to begin with. Vaughn had sent me there for a reason. But the handler and Avalie had no connection. So who sent her to the Surf Ghetto? And who would want the two of us gone?

I didn't particularly like thinking of myself as the prey. I was the hunter. That was my job, and I was good at it. But right now, unanswered questions were piling up, and I needed answers before tomorrow.

My phone buzzed. It was Vaughn. I answered, and we both asked the same question.

"What the fuck happened?"

"You pulled a disappearing act on me." Vaughn vented. "Where were you? You were supposed to hit me up last night after meeting my guy."

"She's from the fucking future," I shot back. "What kind of handler are you? How did you not know that?"

"Who the fuck are we talking about?"

I wasn't going to bother with backstories, and playing twenty questions with him was already getting old. "I showed you an immobilizer device, and you told me there was no one registered to it."

"That's right. So what? What went down? Oh, my God! Don't tell me it belonged to surfer girl?" Vaughn's voice was now dripping with mockery. "No, seriously, don't you think that might have been a mildly relevant fact to mention?"

If he'd been standing here right now, he'd already be on his way to the dentist for a new set of teeth.

"Did you check that weapon in your system records or not?" I demanded.

"Of course, I did. *When* are you going to get it? I'm a trained fucking professional. There were no biometrics linked to it," he asserted. "But you should remember that my resources are only as good as what your people give me. My records are not exactly updated daily. So don't blame the messenger, cowboy."

I took a deep breath and went out on the porch. At the house diagonally across the way from mine, a cleaning crew and a glass replacement guy had just been leaving when I got back from the Surf Ghetto. It was quiet now. Tomorrow would be another story.

"Are we done talking?" Vaughn asked. "Because now it's your

turn. What happened last night? Why didn't you return my call?"

"Last night was a bust."

"What do you mean, a bust?"

My gut was telling me to keep what happened to myself. I definitely didn't want to talk about Avalie. Vaughn had already proven useless in getting any information about her.

"Your guy," I snapped. "The one I was supposed to meet last night. Where was he? He didn't show."

"How the fuck do I know what happened to him? He's not exactly the kind of person who keeps a 'Daily Planner' in his briefcase, you know. Oh, that's right. He doesn't carry a briefcase."

"Keep it up and you might find yourself talking to a Tyrannosaurus Rex. I'm sure he'd find your sarcasm delicious."

"Message received, boss. All business."

Somehow, I doubted it. "Where is he now?"

"I'll find out. He likes the money I give him, so he doesn't stay MIA for too long," Vaughn assured me. "But let's get back to surfer girl. You're definitely saying she's a quantum commuter? So, does that mean a little sex on the side has shot your mission to hell? Because that will *not* look good in your report."

I knew his 'all business' attitude wouldn't last.

"Okay, here's what I need from you right now." I asserted. "Ready?"

"Shoot," Vaughn replied.

"Your vagrant informer. I have to talk to him today."

"Got it."

"And Avalie Briar." I shared her phone number with him. "I want her location tracked. I want to know where she is every minute."

"Check." He let out a whistle on the other end of the

phone. "Damn. Do you think your girlfriend got cozy with you to fuck up your assignment?"

"She's *not* my girlfriend. Now do what I told you," I snapped with more than a hint of frustration. I didn't know the answer to that.

The image of her looking over the roof of that rideshare car came back to me now. *Plan on it* were her exact words when I told her I needed to see her again.

Chapter Sixteen

Avalie

HE TRUSTED ME.

He believed me and accepted what I told him.

Xander came right to me and wrapped his arms around me right there in the driveway. In one moment, he created a comforting cocoon of warmth that spoke volumes. There was no need for more words.

Leaping back fifty-six years, I had no clue how this first meeting would go. I only understood my grandfather as I knew him in my own time. As an old man, his one goal in life was to protect his family. Xander didn't trust people easily. He didn't allow strangers to get close.

Our family was small and tightly knit. My grandfather liked it that way. He preferred situations that he could control.

My grandmother Nadine was more free-spirited, but she also fretted over strangers who looked at us with too much interest and kept a watchful eye for anything that might be lurking in the shadows. Still, she was always quick to laugh off my questions about her childhood. Rarely would she give a straight answer. That was until I was accepted into the quantum commuter program. That's when she finally shared the truth.

Throughout my teenage years, my understanding of her was limited to the anecdotes of their shared past. It seemed that the part of her life she was most open to discussing was the one that began with Xander. The story of their chance meeting and immediate love affair in Las Vegas was a familiar one, but the second encounter a few years later was both odd and vague. A snowstorm, an elk, a winding Colorado mountain road, and a first-edition Jane Austen novel all played mysterious roles in that narrative. As she began to recount the tale, she would often trail off, and the two of them would simply exchange affectionate glances, enveloped in a shared, unspoken connection.

It wasn't until the end of last year that the mystery was swept away.

The stories I heard then were the only means I had to convince them that I was actually who I said I was. I seriously thought they might reject me, thinking it was a trick to deceive them. Never, *never* in my wildest dreams did I imagine Xander would simply take one hard look at me and take me in his arms.

We stood in that embrace for a long time, allowing waves of emotions to wash over us.

Finally, he drew back and said softly, "Come with me."

I was relieved on so many levels when he closed the garage door behind us.

For one thing, they'd arrived a day ahead of schedule. That gave me an advantage I intended to hold onto. I didn't want anyone else to know they were here. Especially Reed.

Inside of me, I could feel a churning sensation as logic and emotion fought to control my actions. Thoughts raced through my brain about how to ensure their safety and how every second counted. But those thoughts were hindered by the flood of feelings I was experiencing, by the deep connection I had with my grandparents.

Like it or not, as I stepped into the house, my emotions took the lead.

As I followed behind Xander, years that were still decades away opened like a picture book before me. Every moment, every memory, splashed onto the pages of my mind with brilliant colors and exquisite detail.

In my earliest recollections, I was the excited toddler, arriving so eagerly at my grandparents' house. The mere thought of the visit stirred treasured memories: playing games on the Persian carpets, building birdhouses in my grandfather's shop, drinking hot chocolate on the porch, smelling the earthy scents of the stables, and feeling the horses' warm breaths as the monstrous beasts took carrots from my tiny hands. So many unforgettable moments that would live in my heart forever.

As the years passed, I naturally became a sulky and ungrateful teenager, and yet my grandparents' home remained a comforting refuge. Upon crossing the threshold of their home, I would feel my turbulent adolescent moods instantly dissipate. Here with them, I found a safe space where I could freely rant and complain about my parents and my friends and the world. They never attempted to impose their will on me. They never chided me for my selfishness. They never overtly instructed me about what to do or not do. Instead, they embraced me for who I was. When I was with them, I was allowed the freedom to navigate the awkward, hard complexities of teenage years on my own. And I knew they always loved me.

As an adult, I still journeyed back to their door, but it was all different. Each reunion was still marked by acceptance and warmth, but I felt the subtle change in that I was not only recognized as their granddaughter, I was also welcomed as a friend. There was still no judgment, no barrage of questions about relationships or jobs. No frowns about whether I was living up to my full potential. Their love transcended generational labels. In their home, the lines between family and friendship blurred. Instead, I felt myself wrapped in a tapestry of connection that encompassed the entirety of my life.

I cherished my grandparents deeply. The bond I had with them surpassed even the connection I had with my parents. I remember my grandfather joking that the reason we were so close was because we were 'united by a common enemy.'

As I trailed behind Xander through the house, following the sound of my grandmother's voice calling out to her husband, I thought my heart would burst.

At this moment, as kind and warm as my grandfather had been just now, I knew that the close relationship we would share was still one-sided. In the present lifespans of Xander and Nadine, I hadn't yet been born, so there was no possibility of them having feelings for me. They didn't know me. They didn't share my memories. They had no idea how strong the bond was that would develop over the years. They couldn't know how important they would be for me. They would be instrumental in helping me resolve countless crises. And if they didn't resolve them, at the very least they would always set me on the path to a solution and support me every step of the way.

In the driveway, Xander had met and accepted me because he knew the truth about Nadine. I hoped she would do the same, but it was still a risk. After all, my mother was only a baby, and that made the stakes in believing me much higher.

As we entered the kitchen, I fixed my gaze on the woman standing by the counter. Nadine had her back to us and was gently bouncing her five-month-old daughter Layla in her arms. Over the years, I had seen countless pictures of my grandmother and mother at different points in their lives. Layla was their only child, their pride and joy. The bright face of the baby immediately turned toward me, her eyes locking onto mine. And then she cooed.

Xander's gaze traveled from his wife to his daughter and then to mine. Three generations of women were standing in the same room. Nadine hadn't yet noticed that I was with him.

I knew their love story. They told different versions of it, of course, depending on the audience. Layla, I think, never heard the truth of how her parents met. I only learned about it when I joined the highly classified Quantum Commute Division earlier this year. It was only then that I learned that time travel was a reality.

Nadine, an early Scribe Guardian in the Division, had crossed paths with Xander in Las Vegas during an assignment. He'd asked her to marry him. She'd said yes, but then stood him up at the altar.

How could she marry him? She came from the future. Xander was a 20th-century millennial. And Nadine felt she couldn't tell him the truth that she was a time traveler.

Then, two years later, she'd been on an assignment to Regency England to prevent Jane Austen from destroying her writing career before it even started. All she had to do was stop the budding author from marrying a rejected but not forgotten suitor from her youth.

The mission had been pockmarked with trouble from the start. With England and France on the cusp of war, the south coast of Kent was a hotbed of preparatory activity, and every stranger was suspect. To escape a situation of imminent danger in England, Nadine had hidden in a newly built coffin before unintentionally time-jumping to a mountain road in the middle of a blizzard in the Colorado Rockies. It was only fate that Xander was the one to find her.

It was then that she tried to tell him the truth. But once she did, he'd laughed it off. To him, time travel was a hoax. It didn't matter. They fell in love all over again, and Xander followed

Nadine into Regency England where the two of them found Jane Austen.

That was their love story. It was *meant* to be.

And that was why Nadine wouldn't return to her life in the future. She'd decided to stay with Xander in his timeline. Her becoming pregnant not only sealed their commitment but also altered the course of history. Still, she knew that her life would never be safe. It would only be a matter of time before the agency sent an assassin to take her back or eliminate her. In that grim scenario, Nadine would be lost. My mother would be lost. And I would never be born.

"Did you find the diaper bag, sweetheart?"

I quickly wiped away tears, realizing only then that I had been crying.

"No, but I found something else. Or, should I say, someone else," Xander said, his voice thick with emotion.

Nadine turned quickly, her eyes widening the moment she saw me. There was no immediate recognition. I expected none. There was only surprise...and a hint of alarm.

I gazed into the depths of the same expressive dark brown eyes that I knew so well. Even into old age, her face had changed very little from the youthful looks I took in now. She had the same high cheekbones, a well-defined jaw, and a straight nose. At this moment in time, she had none of the lovely wrinkles that would someday form around her eyes and mouth and deepen when she smiled. It was always that warm and captivating smile that defined my grandmother's face for me.

More than her physical features, I admired the poised and confident way my grandmother always carried herself. There was an aura of grace that accompanied her every movement, a quiet strength that resonated with wisdom accumulated over the years. A person only had to be in her presence for a moment to realize this woman's character was a testament to the richness of experiences and her innate spirit.

Erase Me

It always filled me with pride when someone said I was similar to her in this way or that way.

Right now, our hairstyles differed, of course. Mine was cut short, while hers was long and worn in a ponytail. I stood a bit taller and had hints of my father's Irish roots in the smattering of freckles and the reddish tones in my skin. Through the years, I'd frequently heard people say that while my mother inherited all of Xander's classic Persian looks, I bore a stronger resemblance to my grandmother. Maybe that was why he recognized me outside.

I quickly calculated our ages. At this moment in time, she was thirty-six and I was thirty-two. We could easily have been mistaken for sisters. But more than our looks bonded us. We not only bore a striking resemblance to each other; we were both risk-takers and known to be fearless. I had no problem with any of that.

On the flip side, we also shared the genetic mutations that made us susceptible to similar illnesses. What had skipped a generation in Layla had resurfaced in my DNA imprint. It was my grandmother's insistence and encouragement that led me to join the Quantum Commute Division.

When Nadine finally broke the silence, her tone was as composed and friendly as if she had expected me to drop in for a cup of tea. "You and I are related."

"Yes, we are. I am...I'm Avalie..."

A knot had formed in my throat, choking out the words. My gaze fixed on the child, who had turned in her mother's arms to peer at me, a sweet smile creasing her face. Looking at the baby only made it tougher to speak.

My mind jumped to Nadine's stories about the moment when she tried to convince Xander that time travel was real. I was hardly an old hand at this, but as I stood five feet from an infant who would one day be my mother and a young woman who would be my grandmother, raw feelings raced through me.

I took a deep breath and glanced at Xander who, thank God, wasn't so much as batting an eye at the experience. His gaze was fixed on Nadine. As always, she was his top priority.

"I'm Avalie Briar..." I tried to start again, but my stubborn tears wouldn't stop. I nodded at the infant. "I'm Layla's daughter. I come from...I'm from the year 2079 and..."

Nadine handed the child carefully to Xander as she moved toward me. An instant later, I felt her arms draw me into a tight embrace.

"Avalie," she murmured. "I love that name."

Oh, my God.

I wasn't generally prone to crying. Certainly not sobbing. Usually, I managed to keep a tight rein on my emotions. Yet, at this very moment, the act of touching, smelling, and holding the person who had always been my anchor—the one I'd loved and adored my entire life—was my undoing.

Hugs were Nadine's secret power, my mother always said. As I grew up, I came to believe it too. Having her arms around you wasn't just a bandage. It was a cure for hurt feelings, breakups, angry words, and disappointments, along with the cuts and bruises that accompanied growing up as an active child. I cherished her hugs. She was never quick to let go. She had no fear of holding you too long or intruding in your space or somehow impinging on your independence. Her hugs were all about love, caring, and letting me know that she was there for me. Always and forever.

I felt it now. All of it.

Love is timeless.

I don't know how long we stood there like that. Neither of us wanted to let go, and it was only the baby's complaints about being neglected that prompted Nadine to release me and take Layla from Xander.

"I have a million questions," he said as the baby settled in Nadine's arms. He then put his arm around the two of them.

"Yes," I said quickly. "Of course."

The family reunion sparked the fear that I was on the verge of losing them. My focus intensified, sensing a genuine urgency in the situation that lay before us.

As my gaze shifted toward the western windows of the house, I noticed a couple of shades had already been drawn back, allowing the sunlight to pour in.

"You're back a day early. That's good, so long as no one knows about it."

"Are Nadine and the baby in danger?" Xander asked, his expression darkening as he traced the direction of my gaze. He detected my concern. He was the same fighter I knew.

"Yes, they are."

"Then we have to go," he said, looking down at Nadine.

"We will," she said calmly, giving him a reassuring nod. "But let's hear what Avalie has to say first."

I'd heard many stories from my mother about her childhood. Xander and Nadine were always on the move. Layla never stayed in the same school for any extended period. She didn't stay in touch with old friends. She was under the impression that it was all job-related, even though Xander was a self-made millionaire and Nadine didn't work outside the home. At some point in time—I guess when Layla was married and I was born —they stopped moving around, thinking they were safe. Safe enough, anyway.

"Running is pointless," I told them. "There's no hiding from them. They'll find you. Your name is on the kill list."

It was harsh to say the words, but it was the truth. And I knew Nadine understood what I was talking about. I walked to the nearest window and lowered the shade to what I remembered it to be.

"That's why I jumped back in time. We have to face them and get their assassin to break protocol."

"I knew this day would come," Nadine murmured to her

husband, cradling the baby more tightly in her arms. "Everything has been so wonderful. Too good to be true."

She was still calm, but her tone now conveyed a mixture of apprehension and resignation.

Xander shook his head. "We'll do whatever we have to do."

"I could still go back."

He shook his head. "That is *not* an option."

"He's right," I said. "Going back is not the solution. Even if you do, they'll target Layla once they discover her existence. In one way or another, she's already influencing history."

Nadine grew pale.

"And by eliminating her," I said. "They erase me, as well."

They both stared at me.

"But I have a plan."

Chapter Seventeen

Reed

WHEN I FIRST ARRIVED IN town, I'd walked along the beach trail, scoping out the area and looking for good places to surf. A few hundred yards north of the San Clemente Pier, the trail passed a narrow valley and a road that came to a dead end at a friendly-looking park. Apartments and beach houses covered the bordering hills. A large play area, grassy fields, palm trees, and picnic tables filled the park.

This was Linda Lane. The beach—a haven for swimmers and boogie boarders—was accessed by way of a tunnel that ran beneath tracks from a small parking lot. At low tide, a person could walk along the water from Linda Lane all the way to the pier. Whether it was low tide or high, though, one could easily walk or bike on the trail from San Onofre Park through San Clemente to Dana Point.

Like T-Street Beach and the other beaches all along this stretch of the coast, Linda Lane had its own personality and charm. Quiet and peaceful, it was a great place for families. It had a neighborhood vibe, in fact.

But not today.

The quiet was currently disrupted by fire engines, an ambulance, and half a dozen police cars and Park vehicles. Emergency personnel stood by the tunnel access and a crowd of uniforms milled about on the beach.

A little more than half an hour ago, Vaughn had texted me, demanding that I meet him here. It was urgent, he said. A body had washed ashore. Someone I'd want to see.

As I drove the short distance from my apartment to Linda Lane, my mind was fixed solely on Avalie. I couldn't shake the feeling that whatever Vaughn was dragging me into, it was somehow connected to her. She'd left me in the Surf Ghetto just six hours earlier—not under the friendliest of conditions—and the mere thought of something happening to her bothered me. No, it was worse than that. There was a twist in my gut that didn't ease up all the way to the scene.

Fortunately, Avalie wasn't the dark, lifeless figure on the beach.

"The surfers spotted him a couple of hours ago, and the lifeguards pulled him out."

We were standing with a crowd of bystanders by a wall overlooking the tracks and the beach. From here, there wasn't much we could see of the corpse.

"How did you find out about it?"

"I've been trying to track him down all day, ever since you told me he was a no-show last night," Vaughn explained, looking out toward the body. "I guess we can accept his excuse for not meeting you."

Why did this guy have to be such an asshole?

"Someone on the beach recognized him as soon as he was dragged out. I think this was part of his regular route through town."

"Who called you?"

"I have my sources. Ears and eyes everywhere," he replied, ego showing in his tone. "I probably got the call before the Sheriff's Department."

"How long was he in the ocean?"

"I don't know."

"When was the last time someone saw him alive?"

"Yesterday, as far as I know." Vaughn shrugged. "I got the word to him to meet you in the Surf Ghetto."

"When was that?"

"I told you, yesterday. That would be Tuesday," he said slowly, as if he were talking to a child.

I took a deep breath and watched as the body was zipped into a body bag. Maybe there was room for Vaughn in there too.

Avalie's warning had lingered in my mind ever since she had walked away from me this morning. Someone had locked us in that shipping container. Of course, maybe there was no *us*. Maybe the poison gas was only meant for me. What if they had been following me, and she would have been collateral damage?

"How did you get word to this guy to meet me?" I asked.

"I have my ways."

"Does he...*did* he have a cell phone? Do you have someone who contacted him for you? How did you do it?"

"What are you trying to do...micromanage me? You want my job?" Vaughn said, clearly annoyed. "Look, I do my part. You do yours. I don't ask about the nuts and bolts of what you do. Don't get into my shit."

As I sized him up, I had to consciously force down my anger. I still needed to work with him on this assignment.

"Okay, let me ask you this. What do you think happened to him?"

On the beach, they were lifting the body onto a stretcher.

"Drowned."

"Foul play?"

"Maybe. It happens." Vaughn shrugged. "But they're having a record year of homeless deaths in the county. They drown. They get hit by cars. They jump in the way of trains on the tracks...when the train is running. Then there's the overdoses. A lot of those. And sickness. The State expects that by the end of the year, between 8-10% of the county's homeless population will be dead."

"Look, Vaughn. I don't need statistics. I want information about your contact. You said he worked for you. I want to know how he died and if his death is related to the job I'm scheduled to do tomorrow."

"Well, unlike you guys, I can't just time-hop whenever I feel like it and fetch police reports a week or a month from now and zip right back here pronto with all the details. I'm a mere mortal, buddy. A living, breathing 2023 guy. I'm damn good at what I do, but I'm limited in how much information I can gather and how quickly I can come up with it."

Everything about Vaughn was starting to get under my skin. The fucker had a chip on his shoulder the size of Detroit. For no reason that I was aware of, he seemed to have an uncooperative attitude.

For my entire career, I'd always been the kind of agent that my handlers appreciated. I navigated smoothly through any situation. But Vaughn had this uncanny ability to bring out the worst in me. Our interactions seemed to spark with tension, making every exchange with him more infuriating than the last.

I suppose what bothered me the most was that he didn't care that my hackles were up.

My best course was to simply focus on the assignment and not let personalities muck up the plans. I only had one more day of working with him. Just one more day, I reminded myself.

"What did you find out about Avalie?"

"I was able to tie the number you gave me to a device. The

last ping I got was along El Camino Real. But no signal now. I'm still searching. My people are keeping their eyes and ears open around San Clemente."

I considered a caustic remark about his people turning up dead on the beach, but I held my tongue.

"Have you checked to see if anyone else from the agency was assigned to a job in this area?"

"I did. Nothing in the most recent report I received. Whoever she is, it's possible she's a rogue operator. She's not in any system I can access."

She told me we would meet again, and I believed her. As for whether our meeting would happen on this loop of the gyre or in the future, I had no clue. At this point, all I cared about was hoping that our current missions wouldn't intersect.

"The job tomorrow," Vaughn said, interrupting my thoughts.

"Right. When are the couple expected back?"

"Midafternoon."

"The husband?"

"He'll be with her. But knowing how you like to work, I can devise a situation where he is called away and leaves Nadine at home alone."

"Do that."

If I could help it, I didn't like involving anyone connected to the target. No collateral damage. As for Nadine herself, every agent knew the rules. They voluntarily signed away their lives and pledged to abide by those rules. When someone from my sector arrived to confront them, they were well aware of their options. Thoughts of Volpe crossed my mind. As much as I would have liked to mete out justice to his sidekick madam, I had to let her walk away, at least for the moment.

"Let's aim at 8:00 pm," Vaughn suggested. "The husband should be out of the house by then."

"What's your distraction?"

"Seriously?" He shot me an annoyed look. "Look. You focus on your job. I'll handle mine."

"I'll do that."

"And maybe, between now and then, you can work on your managerial skills. As it stands, they're not impressive."

It was all I could do to hold myself back. I was tempted, *so* tempted, to give him a close-up look at my managerial skills...with a hard left to the middle of his snarling puss.

Chapter Eighteen

Avalie

IT FELT awkward thinking of *this* Xander as my grandfather, given that he was only seven years older than me at this moment in time. The grandparents that I knew so well were quite old. But their personalities were the same as this couple.

With Xander, I had the advantage of knowing both his past and future. He was recognized as a genius within the tech industry of the early 21st century, and I always thought that much of my aptitude in that field had to be genetically tied to him. But even in his old age, he had an innate sense of protectiveness. So it came as no surprise that he already had a backup plan in place—*and* a contingency plan for the backup plan—for the scenario we were facing now.

If there was a threat to Nadine, and the family had to vanish, no one would find them. Nobody.

I had told them of the imminent danger. Someone else had

been sent to force her to go back. If she didn't comply, the agent assassin would eliminate her.

Xander was ready. Staying at the Avenida Victoria house was impossible. They had access to enough cash that they could leave the country and live off the grid comfortably almost anywhere in the world. They had a house in Colorado and another in New York City. But escaping to a faraway place wouldn't work, either. I had to remind them that security systems and bodyguards and distance wouldn't end the threat, even though he had burner cell phones to replace the ones they had, new identification papers, and everything else they might need.

Assassins were trained to pursue. They were hunters, experts at locating their prey.

My strategy hinged on confronting Reed directly and putting an end to the chase. Otherwise, Nadine's name would remain on the kill list, and one assassin or another would eventually catch up to her.

But we needed to be safe right now.

Xander had that covered. The safe house was a secure location in San Clemente, bought specifically and arranged for situations like the one we were currently facing. There was no link between that property and either Nadine or Xander. Even the car he bought for that location and kept in the garage was a low-mileage, 1978 Subaru wagon with no electronic instrumentation and no possibility of GPS tracking.

When the time was right, we slipped away.

The safe house—a two-story, four-bedroom structure perched on a hill in a neighborhood overlooking the north end of San Clemente—had a breathtaking vista of the Pacific. In the back of the house, an inground spa nestled in the privately fenced yard and faced the ocean. The impeccably landscaped surroundings ensured absolute privacy. It came as a surprise to learn that a property this beautiful had been sitting empty since its purchase at the end of last year. Xander was keeping the place ready for situations exactly like this one.

In a conversation my grandmother and I had in the future, she'd mentioned their time at the Avenida Victoria property but made no mention of this place. I learned now that Xander bought it as an investment as well as a secure place to escape to. Their other stays in San Clemente were in the other property. They'd never had to use this one. Until now.

The two knew my plan for tomorrow. Now, all we could do was wait.

The three of us sat on the patio and ate a light dinner, even though no one was too hungry. Layla was sleeping peacefully in a portable crib, positioned just inside the sliding screen door. Xander lit a fire in the fireplace pit, and we cozied up around it. The sun had already dipped behind Catalina Island, but its lingering rays continued to set the scattered clouds ablaze in the evening sky.

As expected, Xander and Nadine had so many questions about me and my parents and what brought about this jump in time. Their curiosity was measured, of course. They understood time travel and expected with justifiable concern that someone from the future might appear one day.

It was a difficult conversation to get my head around. Only late last year, it was my grandmother—the older version of this very woman—who had blown my mind when she told me for the first time that an alternate world existed in which my mother and I didn't exist. When she'd traveled and decided to stay with the man she loved, the established 'past' had transformed. Family history had been rewritten, and my mother and I came to be.

Xander understood the mind-blowing aspect of time travel. He leaned forward and turned down the gas in the fire pit.

"I was truly skeptical, but then I found myself chasing after Nadine to a time and place I could barely conceive of. I still find it hard to believe at times." He shook his head. "But what's even more unbelievable is how bad Regency England smelled."

Nadine punched him in the arm lightly and they both laughed. "For this past year, I've had to patiently explain over and over again the concept."

"Well, sort of patiently," he teased, giving me a wink. "But seriously, it still blows me away. And seeing you standing in our driveway almost knocked me off my feet."

He was trying to keep the mood light, but I could hear the emotion in his voice.

I smiled at him. "You recognized me. You trusted me."

"How could I not? Look at the two of you."

Nadine reached out and took my hand. Her mouth pursed as it always did when she was very concerned about something.

"Tell me, Avalie. Are you sick? Do you have what I have?" Her eyes darted toward the screen door. "Does Layla have it?"

I immediately understood. Between this time and my own, science would find the cure for many types of cancer, but not the one Nadine suffered from.

She didn't wait for me to answer. "If you don't know, I have a rare type of lymphoma that wouldn't respond to treatments."

"I know. My mother doesn't have it." I reassured her. "You told me that she underwent testing and remained under the close eye of a specialist for years. But she never showed any of the symptoms."

Nadine and Xander exchanged a look of relief.

"She's fifty-six years old now, in good health, active, and has no real medical problems at all."

She squeezed my hand. "I'm so glad."

"And *you* no longer are fighting this disease in the future, either," I told her.

"I'm not?" She exchanged a look with Xander.

This was news I didn't realize I'd be sharing. Her life...*their* life...would be different from now on. "No. You believed—or rather, you *will* come to believe—that traveling back in time somehow reset the clock, stopping the advance of the disease completely."

Nadine had been raised in a youth home since both her parents died tragically in a highway accident when she was twelve, making her a ward of the state. She received her first diagnosis of cancer at the age of twenty-two after years of having her symptoms overlooked. Unfortunately, the disease carried a grim prognosis. It was a death sentence.

Memories of the long conversations we'd had about it flooded my mind. She'd never disclosed to Layla, my mother, about either the lymphoma or time travel. Nadine only confided in me when I was diagnosed with an early stage of the same disease.

She recounted that in her future life, they'd been on the brink of relocating her to hospice when an administrator came in to talk to her, explaining that there was a new trial that might help her. Nadine jumped at the opportunity. She admitted she hadn't actually been hopeful, but she had no other option. She remembered thinking, at the very least, she could replace one of the animal subjects they used for medical research. A couple of days later, a woman wearing a badge visited her and recruited her to the Quantum Commute program.

"When I got into the program," Nadine said now, "they told me they could never cure me. The motivation for joining, though, was that my cancer could go into remission when I jumped in time. They'd found that cell development could be arrested during the molecular dispersal and regeneration."

"That's right. You shared all of this with me in the future," I recalled. "You said they started slowly at first, jumping you backward only a few minutes at a time...then forward again to your present. For a month, they did this every day. And then another month. You started getting stronger, and they kept it up, month after month. Tests and scans showed it was working."

Nadine nodded. "The reset was permanent."

"You thought that the repeated time travel you underwent in your twenties and thirties was the cure. By the time I was born, you showed no symptoms."

"And Layla didn't get the genetic mutation."

"No."

Nadine looked again at her daughter, asleep in her crib. "Is she happy?"

"Very."

"Married? In a relationship?"

Of course, these were the things that mothers typically asked about. My own mother was no different. It was one of her greatest concerns that I hadn't settled down and started a family.

"Yes. She's married to my father. My guess is they'll remain married for as long as they live. They're very happy. Two peas in a pod. Inseparable."

"What's his name?" Xander asked.

"Callum. Callum Briar."

"Irish?" he inquired.

"Do you have something against the Irish?" I teased.

He chuckled. "No, as a matter of fact, a young Irish woman in Hythe, England, was the one who saved us."

"Deirdre," they both said simultaneously, sharing a smile.

It was a story I hadn't heard before, and I made a mental note to ask them about it if I ever had the chance.

"Do you see them often?" Nadine asked. "Do we see them? Wait, don't answer that."

She glanced at Xander.

"What's the matter?" he asked.

She turned to me. "You said that I'm still alive in your future time, but I don't want to know if Xander isn't. Just tell me more about you and your mother."

"First of all, you're *both* alive and well," I told her. "In my time, you're ninety-one years old, and you still walk two miles a day *before* coming and getting Xander for a stroll around your gardens."

"What's wrong with me?" he asked.

"You're too stubborn to get the hip and double knee replacement that you're due for," I said, motioning towards Nadine. "But she's working on you."

"Stubborn? I'm shocked," he chuckled but immediately grew serious. "But *do* we see you often?"

"You see me all the time, and we see my parents whenever they come to visit. They're living on a horse farm outside of Cork, in Ireland."

"Lovely! Is that where you grew up?"

"No. They moved there just eight years ago. My father inherited the property from his parents, and they jumped at the chance for a simpler life," I explained. "They love it there. The world's climate has seriously deteriorated, but where they live is still quite green. The farm is close enough to Cork City to offer some culture, but their village is small enough that everyone knows their neighbor."

"And where do you live?"

"I live in L.A. You two live in Montecito, near Santa Barbara. We get together almost every week." I felt my voice thicken with emotion. "Your house has always been my second home. You two are my everything."

"Hey, come here."

She stood up and pulled me to my feet. A moment later, her arms encircled me. This was the Nadine I remembered. All affection. Her embrace had the power to make everything better.

She released me from the hug but held onto my hands. As she held my gaze, there were tears on her cheeks.

"But I want to know about you. You're here. I assume that means you're in the Quantum Commute Division." Her voice carried a note of worry. "Do you have what I have?"

"Had. As I said, your cancer seems to be in permanent remission."

She nodded. "But what about you?"

Xander broke in, a fierceness in his expression. "Nadine told me that everyone who was recruited into the program was terminal. Does that mean you...?"

"I went through the genetic testing when I was very young. Nothing showed up. I was just living my life...until late last year."

"And?" Xander asked.

"I had some enlarged lymph glands that were blamed on a virus. Nothing debilitating, but that's when you stepped in." I squeezed Nadine's hand. "You wanted me to go through testing again. See the experts. Get second opinions. In the future, science moves too fast to trust old results. It had been more than ten years since my last tests."

"What did they find?" Nadine asked.

"I have the mutations of the disease. That was the real cause behind the enlarged lymph nodes."

"Any other symptoms?" she asked.

"None. But this was when you told me about your illness. You'd lost thirty pounds in six weeks. You experienced neuropathic pain. Numbness in your feet, legs, and hands. Other things too. I had none of those symptoms. Mine was picked up early."

"With me, it got so bad that I couldn't walk. Every day, I was getting weaker and weaker," Nadine said. "What did they do after they identified the disease?"

"A genetic mutation, not the disease. After undergoing more

tests, including a biopsy, they gave me the statistics. The markers were high enough for an official diagnosis. They also told me that what I had would eventually become terminal." Seeing the pained expressions on Nadine and Xander's faces, I felt compelled to share more. "But I wasn't there yet. It could take a decade before the disease deteriorated to that extent. The doctors said that perhaps by then there would be a cure. However, they expressed doubt, citing the rarity of this type of cancer, and the 'for-profit' healthcare system's reluctance to prioritize the well-being of a smaller population."

"Some things never change," Xander muttered.

"What did you do next?" Nadine asked.

"Well, you were with me. Both of you were with me through it all," I conveyed to them. "That was when you mentioned the Quantum Commuters for the first time. I had no idea there was such a thing as time travel. You insisted I should get myself into the program."

"When I was recruited, commuters had to have terminal disease. They came after you not the other way around," Nadine said.

"True, but some of it has changed. A recruit doesn't have to have a terminal disease, but having it improves your chances of getting in. And you can apply to the program if you're referred by another agent," I explained. "Between what you told me and my own research, I found out that the preferred candidates were the ones who have no family. No parents or siblings or partners to go searching for them. The agency didn't want anyone asking questions at headquarters while a commuter is on assignment. Also, top recruits require a certain level of education, good test scores, and the ability to perform physically. Even though, on an intellectual level, I knew all this, until I made my first jump, I didn't understand how hard on the body a quantum leap can be."

"How did you meet all those qualifications?" Xander asked.

"A background check would have connected you to Nadine. That would have been trouble for all of us."

"Not when I actually submitted my records. Thanks to you, I was taking apart, assembling, and programming computers before I even started grade school. I didn't share this with them, but I've made a pretty good life for myself as a computer hacker. My legitimate way of making money is a martial arts studio I run in Los Angeles." I shrugged. "I wasn't going to shine any light on you two, so I made up a new personal record with no family...along with great references, test scores, and everything they needed. I got in."

"I'm very proud of you," Xander said. It was a déjà vu moment for me. I'd heard him use the same words and tone decades from now when I announced to them that I'd been accepted.

"The commuters used to be organized into specific job designators," Nadine said. "Which one did you get?"

"Well, I'd only completed basic training when I hacked into their system and found your name on an active MIA list," I explained. "I was still waiting for my assignment to a division when I came here."

"You're telling me I made it to ninety-one years old without anyone chasing me, but now they want to disrupt our lives?" Nadine shook her head in disbelief.

"Maybe it's the difference between the timeline you experienced and the one I find myself in. More than likely, it's the consequence of numerous changes to history made by other time jumpers who went rogue and stayed in the past. I just don't know. Throughout my training, there were frequent references to *corrections*. Correcting errors made by the agency is a big deal for them."

Xander frowned. "Wait, you only finished learning the basics and you came back here?"

I nodded, looking at my grandmother. "I had to. You two

had done an amazing job of avoiding detection, but when I hacked into the assignment lists and saw your name, I had to do something right away."

"Did you talk to me about it before reacting?" Nadine asked. "I mean, in the future?"

I didn't want to admit that the moment I discovered her name on the kill list—with an Assassin already assigned to her case—I immediately began planning a time jump for myself.

I couldn't wait. Delaying the jump for any amount of time could have been fatal. If Reed succeeded in getting to Nadine before I had a chance to intervene, there would be no tomorrow for me, my mother, or my grandmother. We'd all vanish without a trace. That was a correction I couldn't let happen.

So I immediately requisitioned devices I'd need, reviewed the manuals, and uploaded essential information into Payam's memory for this time and location.

"Avalie?" Xander pressed, breaking into my thoughts. "Did you come and talk to us before you jumped time?"

Not wanting to worry them with the truth, I lied. "Of course. We planned every step of this meticulously."

The exchange of glances between the two revealed their skepticism. They understood that, whether I was telling the truth about this or not, I was a time jumper from the future. I possessed crucial information unavailable to them. And I had as much at stake as they did.

Nadine gently placed a hand on my knee. "When did you arrive in San Clemente?"

"Saturday."

"What have you been doing?"

Spending time with an enemy I came here prepared to kill. Worse than that, having sex with him. Saving his life when I could easily have abandoned him. Getting myself tangled up in a complex web of emotions.

I was glad the darkness of the patio hid my flushed face.

"What have I been doing? Let me think. Sightseeing. Since I could actually go in the ocean, I tried surfing. Oh, and I managed to stop a burglary at your house on Avenida Victoria."

All of that was true, even if it did sidestep the more personal details.

"Burglary? When?" Xander questioned. "The security system never showed any break-in. When we arrived, I walked through the house. I didn't see—"

"I'm good, Pop," I assured him, using the endearing name I always addressed him by. "That was my plan. Something I promised myself I would do for you two if I ever jumped back to this year or location."

"What plan?" Xander asked.

I turned to Nadine and told them what she'd shared with me about leaving San Clemente due to a burglary and never returning, despite her affection for the seaside town.

"I thought that by stopping it..." I shifted my gaze to Xander. "And ensuring you never found out about it, I could give you a few more happy chapters in Southern California."

He shook his head and then laughed. "And I have the best security system money can buy."

Nadine leaned over, kissing him on the lips. "You're talking to your granddaughter. A genius, like you."

He was still smiling when he turned to me. "How many of them were there?"

I didn't want to worry him with the details, including the fact that my rib was still bruised from the incident. "It doesn't matter. You were in Colorado. The way you explained it to me, you watched it happening on your security system, but there wasn't a thing you could do about it. Calling the Sheriff's Department didn't help either. The burglars were too fast, and law enforcement was too slow. Right after that, you put the house up for sale, and you three never came back."

"That sounds like my Xander," Nadine smiled.

We paused and listened to the sound of coyotes barking in the distance. I looked up at the sky and the million stars above.

"But you never told me about this safe house."

Xander chuckled. "Ha! So there was something I managed to keep away from you, Missy."

Suddenly, tears welled up and leaked from my eyes. I couldn't stop it. If I closed my eyes and didn't look at their young faces, this moment could be any one of a hundred evenings we spent together on their patio in Montecito. As I was growing up, Nadine used a dozen endearments, like *Pumpkin* or *Sweetheart* or *Beautiful* or *My Love*. But to Xander, I was always *Missy*.

"Sorry! Sorry!" I apologized quickly, noticing their worried glances. I shared with them a few stories about the special times I'd had with them, and we laughed together about the nicknames and endearments.

Layla fussed in her crib, and Xander was on his feet immediately to check on her.

"Please bring her out," Nadine said affectionately. "I know it's late, and this will mess up her sleeping schedule. But what are the chances of Avalie getting to hold her mother on her lap?"

Chapter Nineteen

Reed

I SPENT most of Thursday watching the target house. However, despite my vigilance, I missed the couple's arrival.

Part of the reason might have been because my mind was on the untimely death of Vaughn's man. I wasn't a big believer in coincidences, but the drifter didn't strike me as a person who'd spend much time in the surf.

The greater reason, though, was certainly because I was thinking of Avalie. I found myself replaying every moment we'd spent together. Since she walked away from me at noon yesterday, I hadn't heard anything from her. That worried me.

I reached out to Vaughn a couple of times this morning, but he had no additional information about her whereabouts. Her phone was dead, and he couldn't locate her. I sent him the phony social media accounts she'd set up online, along with a picture of her. He reported back a couple of hours later, saying that nothing was showing up so far. He used the excuse that San

Clemente didn't have surveillance cameras on the majority of streets, the way larger cities did.

Regardless of this, Avalie's parting words kept replaying in my head. When I told her I needed to see her again, she'd said, *Plan on it*.

So what the hell did that mean, exactly? Did she mean, plan on meeting today? Tomorrow? Sometime in the future? Or did she mean that our current missions were intersecting and in conflict?

And why the hell wasn't she showing up in Vaughn's information? I didn't want to think of her as a rogue agent.

Around midday, I noticed signs of activity diagonally across Avenida Victoria. The house's blinds began to open and curtains were being pulled back. In the early afternoon, a delivery truck arrived in front, and the driver hurried down the driveway to the side door, carrying a package.

Sometime in the early evening, the lights inside the house began to come on. I noticed a couple of second-floor windows had been opened. From my apartment, I could faintly hear the sound of music.

Vaughn had given me his word that he'd engineer a distraction to prompt the husband's departure. As the sun dropped into the Pacific, I continued to wait patiently on my balcony for Nadine's husband to leave. Finally, an SUV emerged from the garage and moved swiftly up the hill toward El Camino Real. The angle and the darkness blocked any view of the car's interior.

I waited for a few additional minutes before leaving my apartment and descending the steps to street level. Standing by my car on the street, I bided my time until an elderly couple strolled past me in the direction of the pier. As soon as they were out of sight, I crossed the street and made my way towards the house.

From the outside, nothing had changed since the SUV left.

The lights were still on, the windows open, and music playing. Still, I had an uneasy feeling about this. I hadn't seen so much as a passing shadow by a window.

Nonetheless, this was the time.

I strode down the driveway as if I owned the place and retrieved the access codes Vaughn had texted me. Surprisingly, testing the door, I found there was no need for them. The garage door was unlocked. Pulling it open, I slipped inside.

The lights were on. The garage was extremely clean and neat. The SUV was gone, of course, and the only other vehicle was a golf cart.

They only had one car. I thought every affluent family in this period had several vehicles.

I crossed the concrete floor to the door that led to the interior of the house. Once again, it was unlocked.

Trusting people.

I hesitated before going in, the memory of the young mother who'd blithely left her children with us on the beach trail came to my mind. She'd said that San Clemente was a close-knit community where everyone knew each other and looked out for each other.

If that were true, I wondered now how many people might have seen me entering the house and which of them was already on the phone to the Sheriff's Department...or getting hold of Nadine's husband to warn him about an intruder.

It didn't matter. I wouldn't need much time. My task was cut and dry. Nadine Finlay, a seasoned agent with over a decade in the Scribe Guardian division of the agency, had gone MIA after her last assignment. She was well-versed in the rules, protocol, and the potential consequences of her actions. I had a strong intuition that when confronted, she would opt to return. In comparison to Volpe and his extensive list of crimes, she posed no significant threat. No anomalies were recorded in the files and no ripples from her actions affecting history. She hadn't stolen anything, killed anyone, or become a billionaire using her knowledge of the future. My assumption was that she would go before Judicial and likely receive a mild reprimand.

The critical question remained how soon the agency would permit her to time jump…and *if* they would. That verdict would certainly be important to her. Nadine belonged to the generation of agents with terminal illnesses; she needed time travel to stay alive.

But that was not my decision to make.

Opening the steel door, I entered a short hallway that led to a set of stairs. Lights were on down here. Looking up the stairs, I could see the main floor appeared to be brightly lit too. Music emanated from speakers set into the ceilings. The lyrics were about taking a chance. *Choose me. I'm the one. The only one.* Oddly appropriate, I thought.

Standing just inside the door, my thoughts briefly shifted to Xander Nouri, the man Nadine had chosen to stay back with.

Vaughn had provided me with a dossier on him. He was a tech-savvy individual, self-made, rich, brilliant. Despite being relatively young—he was only thirty-nine—Xander was making a significant and positive impact in this decade through socially responsible investments. The man prioritized humanity over profit, and his political inclinations aligned with what would be deemed the 'right' side of history in the future. Those who knew him referred to him as private but down-to-earth in person. I envisioned him as the kind of person I would have enjoyed knowing.

But he was also precisely the kind of man I wouldn't want around while I maneuvered to take his wife away permanently.

How long they'd been together was only a guess. But Nadine's last assignment was in Regency England. She'd successfully completed it but never reported back to the agency. This wasn't a rare scenario, as agents occasionally died on assignment. A sighting of her in this era by another agent had caused her case to reopen.

I guessed that Xander and Nadine had been together for slightly over a year.

A year. Was that enough time to justify risking the consequences and potential prosecution? Could love really develop so deeply in that amount of time? Maybe it could. But was any relationship with another person truly worth the sacrifice of your own life?

Avalie's face popped into my head. How easily our romance could have developed into something more. If I were being honest with myself, it's entirely possible that our relationship could have been as problematic as Nadine and Xander's. That is, *if* she belonged to this decade. There was no denying it. I had fallen for her hard and fast. And remembering how she'd most likely saved my life in the Surf Ghetto, I knew she had to have strong feelings about me too. How long had that taken? Two days? Three days? *Damn it.* I guess that's all it took when you met the right person.

Shit! Why did I have to think about her now?

I pushed Avalie's image from my thoughts, needing to focus on the task ahead. Ascending the stairs with caution, I made a deliberate attempt to move silently, taking advantage of the music's cover. Xander Nouri, an adept security expert, had a monitoring system in place for every room within the house. Nevertheless, Vaughn had assured me that he would deactivate the entire system upon his departure.

The kitchen was empty. So was the living room, despite the soft glow of the muted television lighting the space. On the screen, a hungry and determined lion was in relentless pursuit of a nimble gazelle. Even though the sound was off, it seemed like the rhythmic beat of the current song being piped in synchronized perfectly with the tense chase unfolding before my eyes.

Erase Me

My gaze shifted to the built-in bookcases surrounding the entertainment system. The extensive collection of volumes was a testament to Nadine's years of work as a Scribe Guardian. Her role in the agency had been to make sure the literary works and the authors writing them remained unchanged. While her profession had been to safeguard, it stood in stark contrast to my own work as an assassin.

On the television, the gazelle somehow escaped the claws of the predator. It would live to see another day.

Leaving that room behind, I moved silently through the first floor. Lights had been left on in every room, as if someone had planned this, making it easy for me to see into every corner.

After I'd navigated through the kitchen, a dining room, another sitting room, a pantry, and a sunroom, I was satisfied that this floor was empty.

Approaching the foyer and standing at the base of the staircase, I gazed upward, listening. Nothing. Alert for any sign of movement, I went up.

Each bedroom and bathroom proved to be empty, as well. The music surrounded me here too. By the time I reached the master bedroom, I was beginning to wonder if Nadine hadn't gone with her husband when he left. That would seriously complicate matters.

I pushed open the door to a connecting room off the master bedroom and stopped dead. I'd never expected this.

It was a nursery.

The walls were adorned with cutesy cartoon characters. A crib, decked out in pastel shades, was positioned against one wall, a baby blanket draped neatly over the rail. Small stuffed animals hung from a mobile above it, and a dream catcher swung lazily in the breeze coming in an open window.

I scanned the room. A rocking chair in the corner was surrounded by two side-by-side bookcases filled with children's books. A changing table and diapers in a nearby bin. I glanced into the trashcan next to the door. There was even what looked like a dirty disposable diaper in there.

This was the only room in the house where there was no music.

I couldn't quite wrap my head around it. These two had a baby.

Fuck. This *really* complicated things. Why hadn't that asshole Vaughn said anything about this? He had to know. How could he miss it? It wasn't possible that he'd think a baby was irrelevant.

This was the last room left to check. There was no one in the house. I was pretty certain of it. Perhaps there was a way into an attic, but I hadn't seen it. The way things looked, it seemed that the couple had just gotten in the car and gone. Most likely, Nadine had decided to go with her husband and had taken their little one along for the ride.

I returned to the master bedroom and shifted my focus from searching for signs of Nadine to the photographs on a nearby dresser. Several of the framed images depicted the parents enjoying a moment with their infant. A sunlit beach. A snowy, wooded landscape, the baby snug in a pouch. Others were pictures from before parenthood. There was a large photograph, and I picked it up. A formal wedding portrait. I stared at the expression on Nadine's face.

I had seen her picture in the file, but we'd never crossed paths. Still, that face was familiar. I knew her. *Knew* her. I grabbed another photo. The couple stood at an altar, pure joy beaming from their faces. An Elvis impersonator was presiding over the ceremony. The frame had a date embossed at the bottom. *2022*.

How did I miss this? The high cheekbones, the shape of the face, the unmistakable smile. Suddenly, it all clicked into place.

Nadine and Xander had a child. Their line didn't end here. No, it definitely didn't end here.

As I stood by the dresser, my phone buzzed with an incoming text. If it was Vaughn, he'd have some serious explaining to do. It wasn't Vaughn, though. The text was from an unknown caller.

I tapped open the message and read it.

- *Looking for Nadine?*
- *Who is this?* I typed back.
- *Avalie*

Fuck. Fuck. Fuck. Fuck. I took a deep breath and fixed my gaze on the pictures once more. I was an idiot. How could I have overlooked the resemblance between those two? Maybe I deliberately ignored it. Maybe I didn't want to see it. Believe it. Acknowledge it. It didn't take a genius to figure out the exact connection between Avalie and Nadine.

Avalie had to have gone rogue. The Division wouldn't risk deploying an operative anywhere near an ancestor. Establishing ties with one's past was strictly prohibited. It was a serious violation of protocol. And as an agent, delving into your own family's history was explicitly out of bounds.

Okay, so were they unaware of the connection?

- *Still there?*
- *What the fuck are you doing?* I answered. *What are you after?*
- *We need to talk*
- *You can say that again*

I took a deep breath, trying to compose myself and think rather than let my emotions get the better of me.

- *Where?* I typed.
- *Your apartment*
- *When?* I asked.
- *Now*

She seemed to be one step ahead of me at every turn. I hurried to the nearest window. I looked out at my building. All the lights in my apartment were on. I distinctly recalled turning them off before leaving. At that moment, Avalie materialized on my porch, waving in my direction before going back inside. I ran my gaze over the master bedroom, looking for cameras. Was she keeping tabs on me? Had Vaughn failed to turn off the surveillance system, or was there a second system unknown to him?

I was annoyed. No, I was flat-out pissed off. This type of thing didn't happen to me. I prided myself on not making mistakes. But Avalie had managed to deceive me, and Vaughn was proving to be a disaster as a handler. Once I made the jump back to my time, I'd make sure this would be the last job he ever handled.

I obviously didn't need to worry about being cautious. I made my way down the stairs and went straight out the front door, slamming it behind me.

Nosey neighbors be damned.

I was tired of this, exhausted from trying to guess Avalie's motives. She'd had the opportunity to kill me before but didn't take it. It was high time for a one-on-one conversation. I wanted to know what the hell she was truly about.

Outside, I crossed the street to my apartment and hurried up the outdoor stairway to the door. I wasn't at all surprised to find the door left open for me. Evidently, I was to be the guest, and Avalie was playing host.

Before pushing it open, I caught the sound of laughter inside. Two women were having a conversation, with one of them making a comment about liking boxed wine.

Did she seriously bring Nadine here?

I stepped into the apartment and felt the room suddenly closing in on me.

My heart raced as I struggled to comprehend the overwhelming reality of what I was seeing. Disbelief washed through me like a chill wind. That lasted only a second, followed by an intense mixture of grief and nostalgia. I was filled with an indescribable ache for moments I'd lost. For the conversations we never had. For all the important events in my life that I couldn't share with the woman sitting beside Avalie. There was a lifetime that she didn't know about me and that I'd never had a chance to learn about her.

In that fleeting instant, time seemed to warp, merging the past and present, and the void she'd left behind in my life yawned like some great unfillable chasm.

"You're back," Avalie said, her eyes locking onto mine. "I hope you don't mind that my friend and I stopped by for a glass of wine."

My eyes moved back to the young woman, looking shyly at me as I lingered in the doorway. My feet felt as though they were permanently nailed to the floor.

"Reed Michael," Avalie continued, gesturing to the woman. "Meet my friend, Judy Serra."

Avalie had brought her here to face me. She was here in the same room with me.

The mother I'd lost when I was ten years old.

Chapter Twenty

Avalie

REED RECOGNIZED JUDY ALMOST IMMEDIATELY, and his face took on the look of someone who'd just had his insides kicked out of him.

It wasn't quite the expression I was expecting, and the guilt that washed through me wasn't exactly expected, either.

Then, his gaze turned to me.

If looks could kill...

That was the best way of describing Reed now.

Unaware of the unfolding circumstances and the duel playing out here, Judy rose from the sofa and extended a hand toward Reed. She clearly assumed this was a friendly meeting, probably expecting the same vibe she'd received earlier in the day when I introduced her to Xander and Nadine.

Reed, on the other hand, looked at her as if he was seeing a ghost. The color had drained from his face as he slowly approached her. Judy's outstretched hand disappeared in his. To me, his unease was palpable, but I knew him better than she did. Ironic, considering she was his mother.

Perhaps it was wrong to use Judy, but being desperate I had no other choice.

When I discovered Nadine's name on the kill list, I was cornered, frantic to protect my family and ensure my own survival. Before arriving here, I knew Reed had lost his mother to cancer when he was ten years old. The science and the program she created would eventually save many terminal patients...like Nadine. But the development process was slow, and Judy hadn't had the chance to benefit from it herself.

Still, the meticulous plan I'd devised for this moment now seemed, in a way, so poorly thought out because I'd come to know him. I'd come to care for him. As a result, I felt like a brute for putting him through this pain.

But I still had no choice. And Reed was a professional, I reminded myself, when it came to inflicting pain.

"Can I pour you a glass of wine, or would you prefer a beer?" I asked him, my tone casual, as if there was nothing wrong in the world, and this was merely a friendly visit.

"Can I see you in the kitchen?" he asked instead, releasing Judy's hand.

"Sure." I turned to my new friend, who settled back down on the sofa. "By the way, why don't you take a look at the menus of the places we were talking about and decide where we should have dinner. Knowing Reed, he'll probably join us and insist on buying dinner."

"Sounds good." Judy pulled her phone from her pocket.

I followed Reed as he stomped from the room. From behind him, I could see that the tips of his ears and the strip of his neck visible above the collar of his t-shirt were red enough to be on fire. He closed the kitchen door as soon as the two of us were inside.

He put his face close to mine, our noses almost touching. "What the *fuck* are you doing?"

His eyes had been spewing fire in the other room. Now, there was cold fury in his face. He looked dangerous...no, lethal.

My training as a fighter locked in. I was glad I had that, for Reed was a man to fear.

"Do you have something against me bringing guests to your apartment unannounced?" I asked. "You said you wanted to see me again."

"You know who that is, and I could break your neck right now," he snarled. "Who the hell are you? What do you want?"

There was no beating around the bush here.

"An eye for an eye," I said coolly.

"What the fuck does that mean?" he snapped.

"I'm Nadine and Xander's granddaughter. Layla's daughter. As you noticed, they already have a baby. And as you might have already guessed, I jumped from the same year that you traveled back from."

I let the information sink in, watching his expression, hoping that he would back off. But he didn't.

His cold eyes and stony expression told me that he'd already determined this. When he was walking through Nadine and Xander's house, I'd watched him pick up the family photos in the master bedroom. Then, I texted him.

Xander had an over-the-counter surveillance system delivered to the house earlier today and installed it. It was separate from the main unit and had none of the bells and whistles. At the same time, it couldn't be shut down by an outsider. I'd been able to watch Reed's movement through the house on my phone. That was how I knew when he was out of his apartment, and it was safe for me and Judy to make ourselves at home here. Of course, she had no idea about any of this.

All day she'd gone where I'd taken her, spoken to who I asked her to speak with. The entire time, delighted to find enthusiastic interest in her project. And when the meetings were over, she was totally game to come out with me for a drink.

"I'm here to stop you from murdering my grandmother and cutting off my family line," I continued, satisfied that he was at least listening. "Earlier today, Judy met Xander and Nadine. Also, Xander contacted certain connections he has. They now have everything they need to know about Judy. And they will act if anything ever happens to Nadine and his daughter during their lifetime. Like I said, an eye for an eye."

I knew that was a low blow. Judy would die at the age of fifty-one, and Reed was well aware of it. But I could never show him how I felt about him. As far as he was concerned, I had a heart of stone, and whatever we'd shared meant nothing.

"It's a fail-safe measure, if you know what I mean, depending on what happens now."

Reed looked hard at the kitchen door and then back at me.

I wasn't done yet, though. "But there's another side to this. Today, promises were made. Judy secured an enthusiastic investor for her projects. She might be able to—"

"What projects?"

"Cut the bullshit," I snapped, matching his tone.

A seven-year head start on her work could mean the difference between life and death for the young woman sitting in his living room. According to my research, her ideas weren't funded until her postgraduate work was completed and she was already engaged in research for someone else. By then, she was twenty-eight.

"You know as well as I do that your mother is the brain behind quantum commuting. Her research and her brilliance are the foundation of the program. Without her, time travel wouldn't be possible for decades after you and I have turned to dust. Your father and your brother run the show now, but without her, you're all nothing. It's because of her sweat and blood and brains that the agency was built."

His eyes widened briefly as surprise flashed across his face. Before he could mask it, I saw it. This information wasn't available, just as Reed's connection to the family was a secret. As an active agent in the field, he didn't want others to know of his ties to the upper echelon of the organization.

But I knew. Reed's father had a military background. That was how the agency became so heavily funded by the government. His older brother was a scientific genius, like Judy. By the year 2079, he was running things. Information was power, and I was adept at doing whatever it took to obtain it, especially when my family's existence depended on it.

"What do you want?" he snarled.

"Spare Nadine's life and close her file. And don't tell me you can't. If anyone in the organization can do that, it's you. In return, there will be no revenge. Plus, Judy will be fully funded. In fact, she'll start earlier than before. She'll continue her brilliant work, even having time to get married and have children." I tapped him on the chest. "This way, you and I both live. How does that sound?"

The kitchen door opened. Judy stood on the other side, her complexion drained of color and her eyes wide in evident shock.

"How long have you been standing there?" Reed's question cut through the air, his tone different now. I heard in it a mixture of frustration and concern.

"Long enough," the young woman whispered.

Chapter Twenty-One

Reed

FOR MORE THAN A DECADE, I'd navigated the complexities of this job, experiencing numerous jumps that coincided with different times when my mother was alive.

Although I was particularly adept at thinking on my feet, I always pushed myself to follow guidelines set by the agency whenever possible. One rule I deliberately adhered to was steering clear of any potential interaction with her. This decision wasn't solely due to any blind dedication to law and order; rather, it stemmed from a deep-seated reluctance to revisit the heartbreaking absence she left in my life.

I missed her.

The emotional scar that her death created was still too raw. It never faded, and it never will. I consciously chose to shield myself from the heartache that would inevitably resurface if I were to meet her again.

Losing my mother proved to be a challenging experience.

Like many children, I didn't value her enough when she was around. I always thought she was *just* my mother. I never appreciated that she was the person who tirelessly shuttled me between school, sports, and friends' houses. It seemed right that I should be the top priority in her life, ahead of her work commitments and everything else. It was a fact my brother often complained about, given that he hadn't received the same attention in his younger years.

Despite my father always being around, my mother held an unparalleled position in my experiences and my memories. We shared a bond that was uniquely ours. We communicated in a language that was all our own. So, of course, it was natural that the lasting impressions of her final years were marked by the long and painful struggle she faced with her illness.

Over the passing years, in the wake of her absence, I came to grasp a deeper understanding of who she was. I maintained a profound appreciation for her legacy. As Avalie pointed out just moments ago, she was unquestionably a powerhouse, towering above her peers in the scientific community. But with all of her remarkable achievements, she was always, to her very core, my mother. Giving birth to me at the age of forty-one, she was determined to be there for me in a way she hadn't been a decade earlier when my brother was born.

And then, Avalie dragged her into my life. To complicate matters even more, it appeared that Judy had been eavesdropping on our conversation.

People living their lives weren't supposed to have insights into the future. That even included the woman staring at me now, a woman who was a pioneer in the development of time travel from concept to reality.

We'd revealed to her the reality that time jumping wasn't merely theoretical, but rather, she was the one who'd successfully created it. Within the agency co-established by her and my father, exclusively serving the US government as its sole client, numerous agents had been enlisted throughout the years. Their mission involved traveling to various historical junctures, accomplishing designated tasks, and then returning to our contemporary era.

Mistakes had been made, of course. Physical objects left behind. Agents showing up in photographic records. And travelers going rogue to live a better life than the one they left in the late 21st century. Some of them were total scum, like Del Volpe.

Leaking information about the future was one of our greatest mistakes, however. It could set off ripples in history that could in turn set off a chain of disruptive events. Even minor slips had the potential to escalate into major catastrophes.

But it happened. And then, perhaps unavoidably, it became one of the Division's primary missions to correct errors that we ourselves had committed.

As Judy came into the kitchen, Avalie and I instinctively moved apart, retreating and pressing our backs against opposite cabinets. We looked like two children, caught in the act of committing some mischief.

Judy's initial astonishment upon pushing open the door had given way to curiosity. She now pointed a finger directly at me.

"So, you're my son." The hint of a smile tugged at her lips. "That's interesting. How old are you?"

"Thirty-six."

Her smile grew wider.

"Seriously, let me explain," I said quickly.

"No explanation is necessary, at least not from you. You'll try to lie to me." She stood in front of me, her head tilted slightly, studying me as if I were a lab rat just released from an experiment. "I heard everything the two of you said."

"What you heard isn't the entire story," I said again,

attempting to downplay the potential disaster I saw looming ahead.

"We'll get to that later. However, meeting you two confirms for me that time travel isn't something you find in a science fiction novel. It's not just a far-out possibility. What I'm working on is a reality."

She moved with a noticeable bounce in her step as she turned and crossed the room to Avalie.

"We've known for years that the laws of physics allow for chronological hopping—or time travel—but the devil has always been in the details," she said, her hands gesturing in the air. "Time's progression is dependent on the speed that we are moving. The faster we travel, the slower seconds pass. Do you understand what I'm saying?"

Judy waited until Avalie gave a nod in response, and then she began pacing.

"If someone were able to stand near the edge of a black hole, where gravity is exceptionally intense, only a few hours might elapse for them while a millennium unfolds for someone on Earth. Now, when they return to our planet, that individual would have essentially traveled—if 'traveled' is the right word—to the distant future." She looked from Avalie to me and back again. "That is an actual phenomenon, entirely uncontroversial. It is accepted and part of mainstream scientific teachings."

I didn't interrupt or try to distract her. The time for denial had passed. In this apartment, on this night, a shift in history had happened. Judy understood she wasn't chasing her tail with the research she was doing. And, as Avalie pointed out, her work now had the potential of progressing at a much faster pace.

It occurred to me that what had just happened had not significantly changed the larger historical picture, however. After all, we were still standing here. That was a good thing.

And for the first time tonight, the importance of what

Avalie was trying to tell me struck me. Undoubtedly, there was now an alternate future in store for Judy. Could it be that her research would go from theoretical to actual application sooner, allowing her to benefit from her own work regarding her cancer? Could she become an agent in the Quantum Commute program herself?

Was it possible that I'd have my mother around longer as I grew up?

The complications of this scenario were not lost on me, either. My father would never remarry unless my parents divorced, potentially affecting the existence of my two half-sisters. And, my brother, who had taken charge of the company in his mid-twenties, might find more time for his true passion—doing research in the laboratory. All of these personal reasons loomed large as factors in this equation. Never mind the hundreds of other indirect players somehow linked to the original line of history. Some people would live, others might never be born, and countless lives would be forever altered.

It was already too late to change anything about it. This glitch tonight was irreversible unless I took immediate action. An agent needed to travel back in time to a week ago. Avalie would have to be stopped. Judy could never connect with Avalie and learn about time travel. The responsibility for all of this rested on me. I had to initiate the necessary steps. The question remained, *Would I?*

"Are either of you physicists?" Judy asked.

Avalie and I both shook our heads.

"Too bad."

At the age of twenty-one, Judy was deeply engrossed in her scientific work. At this very moment, thoughts about marriage and children—despite me standing right in front of her—were on a back burner. The research she was doing was her baby. It was the only thing that she cared about.

"Other researchers have already created models of time

travel. One involves a wormhole, a tunnel in spacetime that connects one point in the cosmos to another. Sort of a shortcut through the universe." She resumed pacing, her words now directed as much toward herself as at us. "Imagine accelerating an object at one end of the wormhole to somewhere near the speed of light and then sending it back to where it came from. Those two ends of the wormhole are no longer chronologically in sync. One is in the past; one is in the future."

She turned to each of us and smiled encouragingly, as if saying, *Are you keeping up?* I was, of course, but the main thought going through my mind right now was that I was witnessing what it felt like to be in the presence of a genius. This was the woman who, years from now, scientists in the organization and beyond would rave about for her unparalleled brilliance. An older version of this face I was looking at was depicted in a painting adorning the boardroom of the company. The most recent research building at our headquarters bore her name. And, above all, she was my mother.

Judy was gesturing with her hands, creating a model and explaining. "Now, if you're the object moving between these two points, you're time traveling."

Her phone dinged with an incoming text, and she took it out of her pocket. As she read the message, it occurred to me that her research would shift to an understanding of the gyre-like loops within the walls of those wormholes, but she was still years from that. At least, she was until tonight.

Judy was frowning at the text on her phone. She shook her head and buried it deep in her pocket again.

"Okay, now I need you two to answer some of my questions." She started heading out of the kitchen but then motioned to me. "Reed, open another bottle of wine. It's going to be a long night."

I watched her vanish through the door, my gaze lingering even after she had gone. Turning to Avalie, I frowned. "This is your doing. You brought her here. Now, I have to figure out how to fix it."

"No, you don't. Let it be. Some things are better when they're rewritten. Some people are worth saving, worth keeping." Her voice shook. As she spoke, her eyes reflected the intensity of her emotions. "You know as well as I do that history isn't a linear progression of events, where one thing must absolutely lead to another, cause-and-effect. There are many scenarios and more possibilities. It's time you opened your eyes and recognized some of them. Let her live, Reed. Let Nadine live!"

With a fierce glance that told me to consider my choices wisely, Avalie left the kitchen.

I turned around and slapped both hands on the counter. This wasn't the way today was supposed to go. My job, my mission, was to be the hunter—to go after people who made a ripple in history, to stop their actions from becoming a wave.

Despite my frustration over this shift, a spark of hope flickered within me. What if this meeting with Judy became a catalyst for substantial good in the future? Not long ago, I'd discovered that her work in physics wasn't pigeonholed to time travel. She held a wealth of unexplored ideas—concepts my brother was also interested in but couldn't delve into since he assumed leadership of the company. Areas like renewable energy, quantum computing, medical imaging, environmental monitoring, and countless other fields. And then there were the personal reasons for having her around…for me and for our family.

I grabbed two bottles of wine, red and white. I paused at the kitchen door and did a mental calculation, trying to recall if Judy was old enough to drink in 2023.

Chapter Twenty-Two

Avalie

THE MORE TIME I spent with Judy, the more I found myself drawn to her. She wasn't just smart, but personable too. And she also had a certain social grace. She was a person who was comfortable in her own skin, obviously happy with who she was.

Earlier today, during our meeting with Xander and Nadine, Judy had shifted into sales mode, thinking she needed to pitch her research to impress them and secure funding. Others she'd approached had been openly skeptical of the ideas she was promoting. Little did she know, my grandparents were already on board with the idea. All she had to do was name her price; they were more than ready to fund her work.

It was fascinating to witness Judy's transformation into a more confident version of herself just a few minutes ago. She was an absolute firecracker. Once she grasped who Reed and I were and comprehended our background and the journey that brought us here, she became a different person. Now she held the upper hand, and she planned to use it. I had a feeling she wouldn't let us leave alone until she got the answers she was after.

As I sat on the sofa, waiting for Reed to join us, Judy paced the room with restless energy, clearly preparing. Every few seconds, she sent me a sidelong glance, making sure I hadn't vanished. At this point, she had no idea of how time travel worked or what method we used to get here. Only a day ago, she couldn't have fathomed meeting someone from the future. Yet, here we were. And I knew perfectly well that she couldn't share this news with anyone. As Xander had reminded me earlier, if you made this kind of claim to the unwary, they'd think you were out of your mind.

Glancing toward the kitchen, I hoped Reed wouldn't limit himself to wine. I could use something stronger.

I'd laid out my cards with him, expressing what needed to be said. My entire plan was now in motion. I had nothing else up my sleeve. Now, it was Reed's turn. He would either accept or reject my demand. Yet, the nagging truth remained that everything I had accomplished this week could unravel in the blink of an eye if he chose to reset the clock by sending an agent or going himself to an earlier time.

My entire existence teetered on the edge, hanging on Reed's decision to spare Nadine's life. The threats I had made against Judy and the surveillance plans Xander had for her felt pointless now. I knew that. Reed knew that.

The simple maneuver of a time traveler landing here earlier than me could change the circumstances. They could make it impossible for me to locate Judy, no matter how hard I tried. But even more than that, Reed was now aware of my identity. He could intercept me at the very moment I joined the agency, before I ever had a chance to come here.

No matter how I analyzed the situation, Reed held nearly all the cards. Yet, there was one exception—I could resort to extreme measures, even eliminating him. And I was still willing to take that step if necessary. I'd always had a tough time trusting someone else with my life.

Still, eliminating Reed wouldn't resolve the issue of the kill list. Nadine's name would stay on it. If Reed didn't return, other agents would likely be tasked with finding out what happened to him and assassinating her. I couldn't know if I'd have another opportunity to jump time and intervene before they captured Nadine. One thing was certain, because of Judy I would lack any leverage with another agent like I had with Reed.

I was counting on him to make the right choice. My greatest hope rested on the possibility that he would feel an emotional bond with his mother and be motivated to do the right thing.

The stress that had been weighing heavily on me was briefly interrupted when Judy halted her pacing and directed her gaze at me. "So, Avalie, what do you do?"

"Grant writer?" I ventured.

She responded with an eye roll and a dismissive wave of her hand, signaling for me to give it another shot.

"Truthfully, I'm terrible at picking careers. To my parents' great disappointment, I could never see anything through to the end, especially when it came to academics. I've got two half-finished degrees with no diploma to brag about."

She chuckled, shaking her head. "You're here, so you obviously have a great deal going for you. So, spill it. What do you do? Or should I ask, what you are good at?"

"Well, computer hacking and teaching martial arts classes keep the lights on," I confessed, acknowledging my professional side. But then, thinking deeper, I delved into who I truly was, what motivated me, and why I kept moving ahead, putting one foot in front of the other. "But as a person? I'm a born rebel, I guess. Definitely an outsider. I'm comfortable moving on the fringes of society. That's been my life. But I'm also ferociously protective of my family."

I paused, allowing unexpected emotions to wash over me and then subside. I needed to maintain enough composure to speak without falling apart. Coming to San Clemente in this period had proven to be far more emotionally taxing than I had ever expected. Meeting Nadine and Xander, and actually holding my mother—these experiences had raised the stakes sky-high. It wasn't that I hadn't loved them before; I'd always cherished my entire family, including my father. However, after last night and today, I felt a deeper connection with the individuals they used to be. Whatever bonds we shared before, they were infinitely stronger now. The thought that they might not have the chance to live out their lives seemed even more tragic. These concerns weighed heavily on me, and these thoughts didn't even include the reality of my own future, which would be nonexistent.

If Reed erased Nadine, he would also erase me.

"My love runs deep, but I suppose I'm also what people in your time would label as a radical. In the future I come from, the system has failed humanity on so many levels. Those who dare to speak out against social injustice and inequality often face severe consequences. In my own way, I try to make a difference."

"Is that where hacking comes in?" she asked.

I smiled. "Oh, yes. No system is safe from me."

"That's very interesting. I've never met a professional hacker in person before. Tell me some of the things you're an expert at." She shook her head and held up a hand, stopping me from answering. "In our society, and the eyes of most people and, of course, the law, hacking and hackers are seen as a growing problem. But I'm fascinated by the future, and there's absolutely no judgment in this. So, I hope you don't mind me prying."

"I get it. And I don't mind." I was never one for bragging. But right now, given the situation, and knowing Judy's future, this felt more like a casual conversation between two friends.

"Some things haven't changed. The government in my time sees hacking as disruptive, and it is often exactly that. I engage in nano-technology sabotage to stop intrusive surveillance. I use biometric exploitation to forge personal identities for other outsiders. I also create virtual identities through AI manipulations." My thoughts drifted to Payam and how I'd fallen short in that department. I should have been smarter about the encryption and the shields. "And a bunch of other things. Believe me, you don't want to get me started. I'll be talking all night."

"Let me tell you," Judy asserted. "In this day and age, no four-year, nine-year, or post-doctoral degree work will make you an expert on what you do."

"Maybe, but I'm guessing none of those degrees tend to put someone in jail, either." I shrugged. "On the positive side, look at how far it's brought me."

"All of this is impressive," she replied, smiling.

"One more thing. Above all else, I'm a fighter. I'll go to the ends of the earth to protect the people who mean everything to me."

"Are you talking about Xander and Nadine?" she asked.

Judy was no slouch at putting things together.

"Nadine is my grandmother."

"And that adorable baby?"

"Layla. She's my mother. That's why I'm here."

Reed's voice cut in. "Avalie is trying to stop me from taking Nadine back to the future, where she belongs."

I shifted my gaze toward the kitchen. There he stood in the doorway, holding two bottles and some glasses. Our eyes locked, and a palpable tension hung in the air, intensifying the room's temperature.

"But that's not all that you do, is it?" I said coolly.

He glared at me, clearly not thrilled to offer a more candid portrayal of his job. I could do it for him. *I am an assassin. Directives are handed down, and I execute them to the letter. When I arrive, there is no negotiating. You either comply with my orders or you die. I'm a tool of authority...reason and common sense be damned.*

A mask had settled over Reed's face. This was not the man I first met, not the man I shared intimate moments with, and even entertained romantic thoughts about. At this moment in time, it was impossible to know which way he was leaning with regard to Nadine. Or Judy, for that matter.

"So tell me, son. What *do* you do?"

The word 'son' almost cracked me up, but I resisted the urge to laugh. Judy's face remained serious, and the same tone and attitude she'd directed at me were now focused on Reed.

"I correct the problematic blips in history," he said, coming over and depositing the bottles and glasses on the table.

"And how do you do that?" she asked.

However, before he could respond, Judy's phone buzzed once more, shifting her attention. She read the message; her brows drawn together in obvious concern. Then, she glanced up at the two of us.

"I don't understand these messages. He emailed me earlier, and now he's bombarding me with texts. Do either of you happen to know someone named Vaughn?"

I didn't. However, that didn't carry much weight, given that outside of this room, my family was the sole connection I had with this period in time.

Reed's reaction was quite different. His face flushed with evident anger as he reached out his hand. "May I see it, please?"

Without hesitation, she handed him her cell.

"Who's Vaughn?" I asked him.

"My handler," he responded.

"Your handler?" Judy asked. "What does that mean?"

Reed and I exchanged a glance, both of us reluctant to share more information at the moment. To me, it was evident that he was as perplexed by the texts as Judy was.

"Why does he keep contacting me? How does he even know me?"

"That's what I'm trying to figure out," he said under his breath.

I appreciated this noticeable shift in Reed's attitude. Despite his lingering anger, for once I didn't appear to be the cause of it, and his frustration wasn't directed towards me.

"How does he know Judy?" I repeated her question. "Why does he have her number? What is he saying?"

Earlier, Reed looked like he'd seen a ghost when he came into his apartment. He'd clearly had no clue about my intentions or about Judy being here. So then, how could his handler know about us?

Unless...

I knew Payam had been hacked. That was one reason that I ditched my phone. But my AI assistant knew about my plan to meet up with Judy today. Payam also had Judy's contact information.

"What do the texts say?" I asked, pushing to my feet.

Reed scrolled through them, reading them loud. "Hi. Checking on you. Hoping you're having a pleasant day. I'm here if you need anything. Don't forget the email I sent you before. I meant every word."

Judy jumped in. "How many texts are there? Five? Six? He talks like a teenager. A lot of it is total gibberish."

"This is how Vaughn talks."

"What did his email say?" I asked Judy.

"It came just a few minutes before I was supposed to meet with you," she responded, directing her words at me. "He said something about not selling myself short. He claimed to be an investor, and I'd have a blank check for my research if I decided to go with him. I didn't answer him."

I wasn't an expert agent, but I did know that a handler's role didn't include involvement like this. Their primary responsibility was to facilitate the assignment, make local arrangements, and certainly not to possess a higher classification of documents than the agent. On the other hand, I cross-referenced what Judy was saying with the information in Payam's memory.

"So this Vaughn guy was aware of your meeting with me," I said to Judy. "And he had prior knowledge that we were discussing your research funding."

Reed handed her phone back. "Did you tell anyone where you were going today? Anyone at all?"

"Not a soul. Even after meeting with Xander and Nadine. Research money is a difficult business. I've gotten more 'Thanks, we'll get back to you' responses than I care to count. I've learned the hard way not to celebrate or talk about it until the check is cashed."

I turned to Reed. "It seems like Vaughn is taking over. He obviously knows more than you do. I'm convinced he orchestrated both of us showing up at Surf Ghetto."

"How did he get you to go there?"

"Through *my* handler."

"You two are talking in code," Judy objected.

Reed's gaze locked with mine. "How did you get a handler assigned? Your mission was unauthorized."

"My assistant is AI, and he was hacked that afternoon, before you and I showed up in that scrap metal yard. That was a set-up to take us both out."

A new text lit up Judy's screen. The three of us read it simultaneously.

- You'll want to get out of that apartment before the fireworks start.

I heard vehicles pull up on the street, and my eyes immediately turned to the porch. I reached for the nearest lamp and switched it off. Reed did the same with the overhead lights.

Judy showed us the next text.

- Don't believe anything they say. Those two are rogue agents. Come out. You're safe with me.

Reed promptly pulled the young woman out of the direct line of the windows and porch door and sat her by the kitchen door. He moved quickly toward the back of the apartment, switching off any lights. I threw the bolt on the front door, though that hardly made me feel any more secure. One good kick could bust it open, and there were other ways in too.

Right now, I needed to identify who we were facing and how many. The balcony slider was open. Dropping to my hands and knees, I moved through it and crept forward until I could see the street below. Three dark SUVs were double-parked in front of the building, blocking the driveway.

I backed into the apartment. Reed had moved Judy into the bedroom, strategically placing her in a corner by a dresser. I told them what I'd seen.

"I got a text from Vaughn too," Reed told me. "He wants us to send Judy out before we get down to business. And he knows we can't jump time."

One of the fundamental facts of time travel was that after a time jump, another transfer was impossible for at least three days. This interval allowed the human body's cells to recover before undergoing another displacement.

"He knows that's how we were able to disappear from that shipping container Tuesday night." Despite our conflicting goals regarding Nadine and Judy, with Vaughn on our trail, Reed and I were currently united against a common enemy. "We need to face him and his crew head-on, just as we are."

"Why is he doing this?" Judy asked in a small voice, the gravity of the situation suddenly dawning on her.

I didn't know Vaughn. His motives remained a mystery to me. I was just as curious as Judy about what made this guy tick.

"We'll answer all your questions once we get out of here," Reed said in a calm voice, his expression revealing none of the stress I was feeling.

The thought crossing my mind at that moment was that he was exceptionally skilled at what he did. It seemed like he had navigated through situations like this many times before. Or maybe he was just a great actor.

"Then please tell me you two are like James Bond...or Mr. and Mrs. Smith," Judy said with a hint of urgency. Her eyes darted between Reed and me. "Tell me you have artillery hidden in every cupboard, ready to use. I need to know we stand a chance against whatever Vaughn throws at us."

I emptied the contents of my pockets onto the bed, revealing no heavy weapons but a pair of immobilizers. At the same time, Reed reached under the bed, grabbed a smallish bag, and dumped its contents beside mine.

Judy peered over the edge of the bed, examining the devices we had. Combined, all of them could fit in our pockets.

"That's not good. Not good at all. I don't know what those toys do, but we have a saying, 'Don't bring a knife to a gunfight.'"

Another text lit up Judy's phone. All three of us stared at the message.

- Those two are going to kill you. Slowly, painfully, cripplingly, and then wham. They hurt you.

"What is he talking about?" Judy asked.

"He's got oral diarrhea," Reed answered. "And he likes movies."

- What do you say, Judy? How are you going to handle it?

"Is he trying to distract us?" I asked.

Reed vanished into the other room, and I assumed he

intended to assess the number of individuals we were up against.

"Shit," Judy muttered nervously, her voice trembling. "I'm a researcher. I've never once imagined I'd find myself in a situation like this. I hate guns and violence."

"We'll keep you safe," I assured her, attempting to echo some of Reed's composed manner in my tone. "I promise. We're both experts at handling these kinds of situations."

At least he was. But I wasn't going to admit to being new at this.

Reed came back into the room. "The driveway is blocked."

"Anyone out of the cars?" I asked.

He exchanged a hesitant glance with me, reluctant to answer with Judy present.

I nodded knowingly. "You know, you and I can't jump, but she's free to go."

"Where do we send her?" he asked. "And when?"

"To Nadine and Xander's," I told him. "They already know her, and she knows them. At this moment, I know exactly where they are."

"Can Vaughn find them?" he pressed. "Find her?"

"No. He wasn't able to before. He shouldn't be able to now," I assured him. Turning to Judy, I decided to put it to her. "This is going to get rough. You can't stay here with us. Are you up for testing your research way before you even complete it?"

"How about a time jump?" Reed asked.

"Do you even have to ask?"

Chapter Twenty-Three

Reed

DESPITE NADINE WALKING AWAY from her job last year, she was still an experienced time traveler. She'd handled countless dangers during assignments that took her back through scores of centuries. Trusting her in a situation like this was a no-brainer. Adding Xander Nouri and his present-day connections boosted my faith in her even more.

With so much at stake for their family, that couple looked like the best and safest choice for my mother's protection at a crucial moment like this.

Fascinated, Judy stared wide-eyed as we attached a time-travel device to her. Though she had a million questions, time was a luxury we didn't have. A moment later, she was gone.

As soon as she disappeared, Nadine and I faced the grim reality of our situation. I'd seen eight people outside of the cars downstairs, and there was no telling how many more were lurking in the shadows.

"What does Vaughn want?" Avalie asked.

"Money and power, I assume. It fits with his personality."

"Don't you guys pay well enough?"

"He gets paid plenty. Trust me. More than you and I make."

I thought of Del Volpe's wealth, and it struck me that if I were to disappear, those financial assets might just magically find their way into Vaughn's accounts. In our business, a lot had to operate on trust, especially with handlers. It wasn't like we had auditors going around checking books. Unless I raised a complaint or tagged him as a potential problem, dishonesty could become his new favorite pastime. He could skim what he wanted or take it all. Trust in our world was a bit like leaving your wallet on the table and hoping the cat didn't develop a taste for leather.

"Then why is he doing this? What's motivating him?"

"My guess is that he wants a little extra, extra, extra cash. Or a side gig working as an evil mastermind."

"That explains everything," she said, coming to stand next to me.

"Are you considering a career change into the lucrative world of villainy?"

"Why not? Obviously, it pays well. And I can have my own army of minions and fancy cars." She smiled. "By the way, who are Mr. and Mrs. Smith?"

"A couple living up the road. They're hustlers who work the business of lawn mowing."

She elbowed me in the chest. "Can't you give me a straight answer?"

"You seriously don't know who they are?"

"Would I ask if I knew?"

"You've been doing this...let's see, since Sunday? So, you knew nothing about the era before coming here."

"Hey, give it up. I did what I had to do."

She brought her face close to mine, and I found myself

staring at her lips. For a split second, I almost gave in to the urge to kiss her. How quickly I was forgetting what she'd done to me.

"Come on. Who are they?" she asked again.

"It's a movie. They're a married couple who live in a normal neighborhood while juggling covert spy missions with domestic bliss. They don't even know their partner is an assassin. Somehow, they manage to keep their garden weeded and their impressive stash of weapons hidden."

"Move over, James Bond. The real action's happening in suburbia."

"And you know who James Bond is?"

"Of course, I do. At least, I've heard his name."

"But nothing more of the social or cultural history of this decade," I commented.

"No need to be critical," Avalie grumbled, casting me a sidelong glance. "I had Payam to fill me in with that info."

"Oh, your hacked assistant. A real prize."

"Huh! At least, I have an excuse. I was working with an AI entity. How about you and your handler—the underpaid, evil Mr. Vaughn."

"I didn't choose him," I reminded her. "He was assigned to me."

"Excuses, excuses." She perched herself on the edge of the bed and sifted through the items I'd taken out of my bag.

Seeing her there triggered the memory from this past Sunday. That day, neither of us were thinking of weapons or kicking ass. Sex was the only thing going on in my mind, and it was hot. I hurriedly pushed the memory away, forcing my brain to switch off the flashback urge.

Focus on the weapons, I told myself. Avalie had only a couple of immobilizers. Obviously, she believed in quality over quantity. Meanwhile, my collection was a gadget lover's dream. With this, I was prepared for any situation that might rival a high-stakes, sci-fi battle.

Unsure if Vaughn was planning to throw a small army at us, or just make it a lively party, my strategy was simple—pocket what I could. You never knew when a high-tech gizmo might save the day, or at least make for a flashy exit.

"You have more toys than I do," she said, looking a little wistful as she took stock.

"That's one of the benefits of graduating from the School of Legitimate Training. They give you these babies when you have the title of Bona Fide Agent and go on authorized assignments." I may have been smirking a little. "I earned these toys."

There I was, sounding stern, but I was worried about Avalie. While it was true that I'd been trained to handle situations like this, she was walking into a minefield. In this world, without proper training, she was practically a danger magnet. And anything could happen in the next few minutes. We didn't know what these goons had been assigned to do. We could be looking at a hail of bullets coming our way.

Damn it! If there was only some way that I could transport her to somewhere safe.

"Cut the lecture, Mr. Goody Two-Shoes." She cast a glance toward the door. "Before Vaughn and his friends break in, show me your tricks. What do these things do?"

I glanced at Judy's phone. Vaughn was *still* writing texts to her. I decided to play along and shot back a response, hoping to buy us some time.

Next, I lined up my weapons on the bed like a mad scientist displaying his prized experiments. "Most of these babies are biometrically synced to me. I'm the only user. Just a couple of them aren't."

"Well, I plan to be your shadow, so explain away."

She'd better be, I thought. I motioned to the first gadget, a short tube, slightly larger than her immobilizers.

"This contains nanobot swarms. Picture this, tiny nanobots morphing into blades, darts, shields, or whatever else we need. This is the Swiss Army knife of espionage." I pocketed the tube. "But it's more for outdoor situations."

"Okay, save it for that," she muttered. She pushed two marble-sized devices my way. "What are these?"

"EMP Grenades. Tiny packages of joy that emit electromagnetic pulses, rendering electronic devices useless in the vicinity."

"Let me take a wild guess. Another addition to your outdoor weaponry collection?"

"You got it." I put them in my pocket. "Because the Division apparently thinks I only operate in the great outdoors."

"Now we get the truth," she quipped. "You're allergic to indoor assignments."

"Not always," I replied, pulling the next weapon closer. "Enter the Smart Dust Explosives. Does exactly what it says on the packet. Oh, and it's biometrically tied to yours truly."

As she reached for the next device, I snatched it from her hand. "Mine."

"What is it?" she asked.

"Electroshock ring. This baby is armed with miniature, non-lethal electrodes for those up-close-and-personal combat moments."

"Really?" Avalie shook her head in disbelief. "You need a gadget for that too? What happened to good old-fashioned street fighting?"

She definitely had a massive attitude. Recalling how she'd effortlessly flipped me in that storage container a couple of nights ago, I judged she had some experience in martial arts. But that night she had the element of surprise on her side. I didn't expect her to be there. And when I saw her, my first reaction was to trust her. Whatever was going to happen here in this apartment, she could be out of her league.

Time was running short. I grabbed the next device. "This thing unleashes an expanding sonic cone that will either disorient or turn our opponents into interpretative dance enthusiasts."

"Looks like it would be too complicated and slow to activate," she said, immediately reaching for the next items. "Immobilizers. Wait, these are mine."

"Yes, they are. An older model, though, compared to my state-of-the-art neural disruptor."

"They call them immobilizers. And mine are the same as yours."

"Yours are assigned to rookies. My neural disruptors are the Ferraris of immobilizers. They emit targeted signals that disrupt neural pathways, causing temporary paralysis or confusion."

Avalie scoffed. "Mine do the same thing. And I recall my device knocking a certain someone right on their ass." She pocketed hers. "Get us out of here alive tonight, and we can settle this with a good old shootout."

"Let's not call it a shootout," I suggested.

She shot me a look that could melt ice. "I don't care what you call it. My immobilizer against whatever fancy reject you've got in your hand."

"That's a deal."

I had no idea how long it would be before Vaughn's crew came barging through the door. But I liked seeing her looking so fearless and ready. This woman would never be one to hide in a closet or under the bed and wait for the dust to settle. At the same time, I had to figure out a way to keep her safe.

I pointed to the last two items on the bed. "Drone Assassins. Think of these as the James Bonds of the gadget world. They can be used as weapons or as high-tech, mobile surveillance devices."

"Ah, great," she groaned, clearly not overly impressed. "Another complicated piece of techno-crap."

"Now, listen. I've handled this kind of situation before. I'm a pro. You, on the other hand—"

"Are a rookie. I get it."

"I want you to follow orders. Be the invisible sidekick."

"Try not to become a casualty," she added.

"Exactly," I emphasized. "Can you do that?"

"I'll try."

"Trying isn't good enough. I need your solemn promise."

She was probably crossing her fingers behind her back, but she nodded. "You have my word."

"Good." I wished I had a lie detector device handy.

Just then, another text from Vaughn lit up Judy's screen.

"Is he still texting her?" Avalie asked.

"He won't be, after this," I told her, writing back.

- *Fuck off, Vaughn! We're ready for you.*

Chapter Twenty-Four

Avalie

Reed and I were standing on either side of the bed, him still insisting that I sign a sworn statement when something tore through the screened window. It thudded on the floor before rolling under the bed.

My eyes barely caught a glimpse of it. "What the fuck?"

As I reached the end of the bed, a second bang sounded from the kitchen. It could have been a brick taking a nosedive into the sink. A split second later, a third thud came from the floor of the sitting area.

"Maybe you texted him back too soon," I muttered under my breath.

Whatever it was under the bed, it made a distinct click.

"Stay back," Reed warned.

Without hesitation, he reached down, gripping the side rail under the mattress. Driving with his legs, he executed a powerful lift, sending the entire bed right over.

We stared at the object. It was a silver canister the size of a soda bottle. And now, it was hissing.

I recognized the odor, and it sent a chill down my spine. It was the same stuff Vaughn had tried to use on us in the Surf Ghetto. "Gas grenade. I've got it."

"No, *I've* got it. Stay back."

I was closer to it, so we both lunged towards the canister. At the last moment, Reed expertly shouldered me aside, scooped up the device, and hurled it back out the window. I quickly slammed the window shut.

"I could have handled it," I protested.

"I told you to stay back. Follow directions. Go find a corner and stay out of trouble." He headed for the door. "They threw more canisters in. I'll take care of it."

I watched him with a mix of amusement and exasperation. "Do you want me to tidy up in here?"

He was already out of earshot.

"I guess we're not doing sarcasm today," I muttered to myself.

He was in the living room by the time I got out there. I made a beeline for the kitchen door.

"Don't breathe," he yelled over his shoulder.

Oh. My. God. Obviously, I missed the 'Don't Inhale Poison Gas' training session.

"There's another one in the kitchen," I shouted. The hissing sound was unmistakable. "Throw that one in here."

Standing by the door, I held my ground, wondering if he'd actually listen to me or if he'd think he could disable the device with a toothpick.

To my thinking, the apartment had just two straightforward entry points, which gave us a bit of an advantage. Despite a few windows, being on the third floor meant any intruders would likely have to choose between the door at the top of the stairs on the side of the building or the porch slider facing the street.

The door to the right of my current position led to the outside stairwell, while straight ahead, past the living room, was the porch slider.

"Open it," Reed's shout reached me as he hurled the canister into the kitchen from about ten feet away. The gas grenade bounced and skittered by me, and I slammed the door.

The room tilted slightly. I'd inhaled a small amount of the gas, and it was taking its toll.

Reed stood before me. "Are you all right?"

"Perfect. You?"

He eyed the door. "They'll be here any minute. Go to the other room."

"I'm not going anywhere."

"You promised me."

"I lied."

"I knew it." Reed frowned. "Stay behind me when they come through."

"Whatever you say."

"I'm serious. I'm the one trained for this, and we don't know what else they'll throw at us."

Sure enough, I heard the sound of boots coming up the stairs to the landing outside the apartment. "Think any of them will be armed?"

"All of them, probably." He actually grinned. "This is America in 2023, after all."

We were a study in contrasts, wired in our own individual way. After our whirlwind fling ended abruptly, I tried saving my family and myself with a number of lies. The move earned me his resentment, particularly when I involved his mother. Adding to the difficulties between us was the fact that I had contemplated taking him out from day one. On the other hand, Reed had the power to dismantle my efforts completely if we made it through this day alive.

Still, at this very moment, despite everything and against all odds, I found myself deeply in love with this guy. Ice ran through his veins, and honestly, there was no one else I'd want fighting alongside me.

Right then, there was a bang on the apartment, and the latch began to buckle. One more shove and that door would be ancient history.

As we moved to stop them from coming in, two men wearing gas masks crashed through the porch slider. Reed expertly elbowed me aside, positioning himself to confront the intruders.

"Need me to whip up some snacks for your new buddies?" I asked.

"Cheese and crackers would be perfect," he deadpanned, just as the first man lunged at him.

So, sarcasm wasn't off the agenda, after all.

The attacker had the lean, defined muscles of a gymnast. He immediately launched a flying kick head high.

Reed sidestepped and the attacker sailed by, landing closer to me. As he rolled to his feet, I grabbed his wrist and yanked to keep him off-balance. A knee to his ribs doubled him over, and a second knee to his face put him down for good.

Reed threw a surprised glance my way, but then the second fighter was on him.

This one was lithe, quick, and clearly more skilled. The two engaged in a dazzling exchange of punches, blocks, and parries.

Despite my urge to jump in, Reed had it under control. The assailant made a fatal mistake, lunging at the wrong moment. Reed swiftly turned the tables, launching him over his shoulder. The man crashed onto the coffee table, demolishing it and sending wine glasses flying. Two bottles rolled across the floor as Reed delivered the finishing blows with precise chops to the thug's throat.

In a blink, Reed was by my side. "Are you okay?"

"Not if I have to pay for that table," I quipped.

He snorted. Before he could come up with a snappy reply, though, the latch splintered, and the apartment door swung open with a bang.

The first to enter was a towering figure, a giant whose sheer size demanded attention. His broad shoulders strained against the confines of his leather jacket, and his imposing stature filled the doorway.

"I've got this one," Reed said.

"I'm shocked," I replied with a straight face.

Before the intruder could regain his balance from delivering the forceful kick, Reed responded with a swift front kick squarely to the guy's chest. The intruder had a pry bar in his hand that he didn't get to use. The last I saw of him, he was sailing backward over the railing. The drop from the top of the outside landing had to be around thirty feet or so, but I had a pretty good idea the pavement at the bottom wasn't a comfortable landing spot.

The next one led with a pistol as he came in. Bad move.

"Got it," I murmured, already knowing I wouldn't get the opportunity.

I didn't. Reed cut me off.

"Seriously?"

Before the guy could fully cross the threshold, Reed was on him like a tornado on a small town.

A door jamb works very well as the fulcrum of a lever. Grabbing his wrist, Reed cranked it hard against the splintered wood frame. The cracking of the bones in the forearm was sharp, putting the hand out of commission. The pistol clattered to the floor, and with a swift kick, Reed sent it skidding away.

Another goon was trying to get around the gunman, who was currently clutching his broken arm and jerking backward and howling with pain. The two were momentarily tangled up.

Before they got untangled, Reed shoved fiercely at the shoulder attached to the broken arm, eliciting a scream that was probably heard all the way to the beach. It didn't last long, though, because they were playing follow the leader over the railing.

"I'm bored here," I wisecracked. "Give me something to do."

"Avalie," his tone carried a hint of warning. "I told you—"

Before he could finish, two more guys burst through the door.

Reed deftly ducked under a length of angle iron that the first one swung at his head. He drove a fist into the solar plexus of the young bruiser and leveled him with two forearms to the jaw.

The man behind him was small, wiry, and quick. He was brandishing a collapsible baton. Dropping low, he lashed out with it with the speed of a striking cobra. He was aiming higher, but the weapon caught Reed on the side of the shin, staggering him momentarily.

Seeing his advantage, he drew back to take a swing at Reed's face.

Before he could, I got one hand on his baton arm and spun into him. My elbow connected directly with his forehead, causing his small head to snap back. Following up with a swift chop to his throat, he crumpled into a heap in the corner.

Reed began to say something, then suddenly reached out and spun me to the side. I hit the wall at a velocity that didn't give me a particularly warm feeling about the situation. But as I looked up at the new attacker, I had a few seconds to size him up.

To put it mildly, he was a nightmare of giant proportions.

Long greying hair sprouted from beneath a black knit beanie. Standing close to seven feet tall and as wide as a bull, the tan coveralls he wore seemed custom-made by a local tentmaker.

The monster glanced at me, dismissed me as inconsequential, and lumbered toward Reed.

For the first time since arriving here, I was really, really worried. This was a scenario I would have shrugged off a week ago, I realized. Reed was the person I had to protect.

As the giant got close to him, Reed tried a front kick. Not exactly effective. Instead, he propelled himself backward, where he tripped over the bodies of the men we had just taken down.

Reacting quickly, I grabbed a wine bottle from the floor and hurled it directly at the monster's massive head. Surprisingly, I made contact. The base of the bottle struck the back of his skull solidly. That only succeeded in grabbing his attention, however, and he turned, lumbering back across the room toward me.

I'd seen what Reed's kick had done, so I wasn't feeling too optimistic about throwing a kick of my own at him. I thought about his legs, but they looked like tree trunks.

Opting for a more substantial weapon, I seized the steel angle bar dropped by the muscle boy and swung it at the colossal figure.

The blow to his face was hard enough to cause a jump on the Richter scale. The oversized head barely moved, though, and the eyes never even flinched.

"He's trouble. With a capital T," Reed remarked loudly from the background.

When I swung the bar again, he knocked it out of my hand with one massive paw and grabbed me by the throat with the other.

As he lifted me, I felt the fingers clamp down on my windpipe.

Then, Reed was on the giant's back. He had his left arm around the man's throat while he pounded at the face with his right.

From my vantage point—dangling in the air from our

Erase Me

attacker's fist—I got to see the action up close. At first, the monster didn't seem to notice, but when Reed mashed the nose to the side, it got his attention.

The big fellow acted like he'd never had his nose broken before.

The cheeks flushed red with rage and his eyes were on fire.

He dropped me to the floor, none too gently, and reached back for Reed.

I had only one way of helping my partner at the moment. Arching my body up, I kicked him squarely in the balls.

I don't think I've ever seen someone's eyes bulge quite like his did. He sat back down on his butt so heavily that the entire building shook.

With his arms locked around the giant's head, Reed had the leverage he needed to finish the job.

"Nice," I said.

"I knew you could take him alone," Reed said, his voice actually laced with a hint of pride. "But we've got more fish to fry."

I knew you could take him alone. We've got more fish to fry.

It was stupid to feel emotional in a moment like this, considering the urgency of the situation. But I couldn't help but feel a surge of happiness. Whether it was authorized or not, this was my first job. I found myself caring for Reed, and adrenaline was still coursing through my veins at full throttle.

Reed cast a glance through the door to see if anyone else was coming. Seizing the moment, I darted for the porch, scanning the street below for potential dangers. Outside, there was no sign of movement near the cars. Could it be that every one of them had come up here to take us down? More likely, the rest of the hired help had turned tail and run.

Returning to the living room, we found ourselves surrounded by the aftermath of the fight. Bodies were scattered everywhere. The furniture was in splinters. There were holes in the walls. The once-cozy living space was now unrecognizable.

At one end of the shattered table, my eye fell on the Jane Austen book. It sat on the floor, seemingly undisturbed by the chaos around it. I walked over, picked it up, and wiped shards of glass off the cover.

"I meant to drop that off at your new friend's house," Reed commented. "The one from the beach."

"Well, maybe there's still time." I tucked the volume under my arm as memories rushed in. It was because of reaching for this book that Reed and I met. Jane Austen had played the role of matchmaker for us. I reflected on how different everything would have been if we had not connected.

"Are you okay?" he asked.

"Yeah."

As we stood amidst the wreckage, one of the young bruisers groaned and started to sit up.

Reed pushed him back down and placed a forearm on his throat. "Where's Vaughn?"

The thug's eyes shifted toward the inert hulk nearby. Fear flickered in them when he looked back at me and then Reed.

"I'm not asking again. Where's Vaughn?" Reed demanded, his voice edged with impatience.

"On the boat."

"Still in the marina?"

The young man shook his head.

"What boat?" I asked.

"I know the boat," Reed replied, glaring at the young thug. "Tell me where it is now."

Chapter Twenty-Five

Reed

THE BRIGHTLY LIT BOAT—FORMERLY Del Volpe's yacht and now, apparently, Vaughn's—was anchored about a half mile off the San Clemente beaches. The night sky was crystal clear, with only a few patches of clouds to the west. Other than that, it looked like every star in the universe was shining tonight. The pier, just a few hundred yards to the south of us, also glowed with lights from the restaurants on the shore all the way to the bait shack at the end.

I would have preferred a nice thick fog, but that wasn't in the cards tonight.

By the time Avalie and I left the apartment, police sirens were coming from every direction. Outside, Avenida Victoria was starting to look like a holiday block party, with people filling the street. Even though it was apparently true that folks in this town kept tabs on each other, I was glad that didn't include any would-be hero coming up and getting into the middle of the fight.

Having grabbed everything I needed, we went down and blended into the crowd. We acted as if the commotion and destruction were the work of the apartment above ours. And as soon as the first Sheriff's Department vehicle rolled in a couple of minutes later, we made our way toward the beach. Our job there was done. The next chapter awaited.

Naturally, Avalie had her own ideas about things. She insisted on making one stop—in case we didn't make it back. So, we walked through town to the address where Tina lived. I was only teasing her about it up in the apartment, but God forbid that a used copy of Jane Austen's *Pride and Prejudice* should go astray. We left the book on the woman's front step.

That brought us here, kneeling on paddleboards on an undulating black sea, fifty yards from the yacht. We hoped the boards would make our approach less conspicuous.

Avalie was running one hand through the water, stirring up blue foam. "I'm glad I got a chance to see this bioluminescent phenomenon before…"

"Before we leave? Or before we're killed."

"I was going to say, before we get eaten by sharks. Aren't they out here now? Tiger sharks? Great whites?"

She was joking. I could hear it in her voice. I didn't want to tell her that a twelve-foot great white shark had been spotted swimming under the pier earlier this year. The surfers were still talking about it.

That news probably wouldn't make a difference to Avalie. The woman lacked fear. One of a kind, to be sure.

"Keep agitating the water with your hand like that and we'll find out if there's any in the neighborhood."

She reluctantly drew her hand out of the glowing blue froth and watched me finish prepping the drones. They were only the size of dragonflies, but they could be used either to attack or surveil a target. There were only two, and I'd decided it would be best to use them for surveillance of the yacht before we went in.

It took less than a minute to sync them with my phone, and I activated them. The wings spread, and the devices lifted smoothly and quietly off the board. They immediately disappeared into the darkness.

The drones were voice-controlled, and I directed them in a wide arc to the south. I wanted to get a good view of the stern section, where we'd be boarding the vessel. I kept them low to the water, watching their progress on a split screen on my phone.

Avalie was leaning toward me and watching the screen. "Do you think that's a good idea, having them fly that low?"

"I don't want them flying higher until they reach the..."

I stopped midsentence. The image of a fish's open mouth appeared on one of the screens and then that drone went dark.

"Was that what I think it was?"

I immediately moved the remaining drone to a height of a few meters above the surface of the water.

She was clearly choking back a laugh and wisely said nothing more.

The drone reached the yacht safely, and I moved it to where I could see the stern deck and then the rest of the target. Four armed men were sitting on benches on the middle deck. By now, they had to be on alert to the debacle at my apartment. On the top deck, a light was on in the bridge, where I could see the captain.

"Are those grainy images the best that thing can do?" Avalie was eyeing my phone. She waved a hand toward the yacht. "I can see the boat better from here."

"You know, I think sharks are attracted to human voices too."

Just then, a fifth man joined the others on deck. He was carrying a tray with cups of some kind of beverage.

"I take back everything I said about the drone images," she murmured. "Those are clearly café mochas in those cups."

"Let's go."

"Good. I could use one of those right about now."

I grabbed my paddle and stood up. "If you wait here, I'll bring one back for you."

"No way," she scoffed, standing and putting her paddle in the water. "I'm coming. It'll be cold by the time you get back."

We paddled in silence toward the boat, circling around to the stern. The swimming platform was extended, and we climbed carefully aboard, pushing the paddleboards off into the darkness.

Standing in the stern, I realized Avalie was still holding her paddle. When I gestured questioningly toward it, she leaned close, whispering, "This weapon and I are biometrically synced."

"Great. Stay behind me."

Two sets of stairs on either side of the boat led to the deck where the armed men were sitting. My plan was to go up and take them out.

We could hear their voices. I think they were talking about baseball. In any case, they didn't sound too concerned about us.

I gestured for her to follow me, but she moved toward the opposite set of stairs.

There was just no way to control her, I thought as I put my foot on the first step.

Almost immediately, the steward who'd brought beverages before reappeared on the deck between us. He was carrying food on his tray and turned in my direction. When he spotted me, we both stopped dead.

Shocked, he backed away a foot, still holding the tray with one hand, and reached into his jacket.

Erase Me

The blade of Avalie's paddle connected with the side of his head with a solid crack. He wobbled momentarily and went down. Unfortunately, so did the tray he was carrying. I heard the talking stop on the deck above. Then, running footsteps.

I glanced over to see where Avalie was. She was only a step away from me.

Pulling the soundwave weapon from my pocket, I activated it. Then, reaching out for her, I drew her close to me.

Two of them were carrying pistols. The other two had MP5 machine guns. They didn't get the chance to use them.

With Avalie at my side, I aimed the little device and unleashed an ultrasonic wave that exceeded 400 meters per second and directed a silent, invisible, cone-shaped field toward them. It hit them hard.

Weapons clattered to the deck as they clutched at their ears. Immediately disoriented, two dropped to their knees and then fell over senseless. The other two went over the side.

"Thanks for getting me out of the line of fire," Avalie said.

Moving to the top of the stairs, I threw the weapons overboard.

Avalie appeared at my side as I glanced at the men in the water. The cold Pacific must have kept them conscious, but they were still confused and lacking in muscle coordination. Somehow, they were able to keep their heads above the surface.

"All that splashing probably won't draw sharks," she said.

"Probably not."

"Okay, give me something to do."

"What happened to your paddle?"

"It broke somehow. Crazy, huh?" She peered into the dining area.

Not as crazy as what I was feeling right now.

Here was this woman that I'd just fought beside in a pitched battle in that apartment. A woman who'd more than held her own. She'd kicked ass up there. Here was a woman who—with minimal training—had successfully hacked her way into the Quantum Commuter Division and then traveled back to exactly the right moment in time to keep her grandmother safe. To keep her mother safe. To keep her family line safe.

Avalie was capable. Supremely capable. She didn't need a protector. Still, I wanted to protect her. I needed to protect her.

"What now?" she pressed. "Go after this Vaughn character? Where do you think he is?"

I looked up the stairs. "First, we take care of the ship's captain. We don't want him calling the Coast Guard when the shooting starts."

We'd taken out five members of the crew, and the captain would make six. Most of the attackers in the apartment appeared to be hired henchmen. They might have been crew members among them, but I had no way of knowing. The muscular young man who confronted me the night I killed Volpe might still be recovering in the hospital. I doubted he'd be eager to return to work on this boat. It was impossible to determine how many more were presently aboard.

I also wasn't sure where Vaughn was hiding, but I had a good idea. What his next step might be was anyone's guess. But one thing I did know. We weren't dead yet.

Avalie gestured toward the men, out cold on the deck. "Are you going to use your sonic toy on him too?"

I shook my head. "It's a single-use weapon. We have no way to recharge it in 2023."

"I'll take care of him," she said.

She looked away, like a professional fighter straining to come out for the tenth round. She was dressed all in black, which probably hid blood from the guys she'd put down in the apartment. But she had skinned knuckles, a darkening bruise on her cheekbone, and her short hair was a mess. She was fucking beautiful.

And there was no holding her.

"Use this." Extending the electroshock ring toward her, I whispered, "Do it quietly. And be careful. There could be more people on this boat."

Climbing the steps to the upper deck behind her, I positioned myself in the shadow of a bulkhead.

As Avalie strode across the deck and went into the bridge enclosure, I followed, watching like a hawk. I needed to stay nearby, in case she needed me.

I almost went in when a muffled cry reached my ears. But before I could move, she strolled out. From my vantage point, I could see the captain slumped over the controls.

When she reached me, Avalie took off the ring and shrugged. "Well, this thing didn't work. But that guy in there is going to have a very sore neck when he wakes up. Anyway, we're all set."

"Good." I looked away, relief washing through me. She was okay.

I considered scouring the boat for any remaining personnel but dismissed the idea. If they weren't coming for us now, they weren't too keen for a fight. Just to be sure that no one would be monitoring our whereabouts, though, I activated one of the marble-sized EMP grenades. I tossed it toward the bridge and saw the lights on the console flicker and go dark as the electromagnetic pulses did their job.

Glancing at Avalie, I considered leaving her on the bridge until my business with Vaughn was done. However, there was still the risk of other crew members cornering her there. The safest course of action was to keep her by my side.

"Okay, follow me. I have a good idea where Vaughn will be."

Going back to the lower deck, I led Avalie past the galley. There was no sound coming from the companionway that led down to the crew's quarters.

Not far ahead were the steps leading to the passageway

where the cabins were located. The spa and exercise rooms were dark as we passed by. However, only a few steps beyond, I sensed a surge of energy behind me.

Turning, I witnessed a man gripping Avalie by the neck, a gun pressed against her head. I recognized him as one of Volpe's bodyguards. The first one I'd run into the last time I was boarding this boat. The big ugly face and the bad haircut.

Her face was unreadable, but cold dread washed through me.

"I was hoping to see you again, pal," he said coolly, prodding Avalie's temple with the muzzle of his pistol. "Nice of you to bring along this one too. Now, let's go see the boss."

"Glad to see you're not unemployed these days," I said, stalling for time. "Your last boss must have given you a great recommendation."

"He didn't get the chance, actually."

"You didn't tell me you had friends on this yacht," Avalie said to me.

"Oh, yeah," the thug growled. "We're old pals. Now *move* it."

As I considered my options, I felt a jolt of fear that this brute might kill her on the spot. It seemed apparent that these men had been instructed to do just that at my apartment.

"Okay. Where?" I asked.

The bodyguard pointed his pistol toward the stairs. As soon as he did, Avalie reached up and hit him in the neck with her immobilizer.

The man's eyes opened up to the size of dinner plates, and as I grabbed the pistol from his hand, she gave him a sharp elbow in the face for good measure. He went down in a heap. It was all I could do to stop myself from stomping his face into mush.

Before I realized it, I had pulled her close, enveloping her in my embrace. We stood there in silence for a moment, and I felt her arms encircling me, as well.

But then, reality broke through the haze. Reluctantly, I let her go.

"I was careless there. He shouldn't have gotten the upper hand on me," she admitted.

"You did great," I reassured her. "No second guessing yourself."

"Guess my old immobilizer still does the job."

"Definitely. Now, let's go find Vaughn."

It took only another minute to reach the stairs that led up to the row of cabins. We went straight up. Surprisingly, the stateroom door at the far end was open.

Moving cautiously past the closed doors, we were only a few feet from the main cabin when a voice called out to us.

"Come in," Vaughn said. "I don't want you bozos doing more damage."

He was standing by the opening in the outer wall of the stateroom. The open-air balcony was empty of the furniture that had been there when I confronted Del Volpe. An MP5 machine gun lay on a side table.

"Time to behave, kids. Act civilized."

My first thought at that moment was *when* had he placed the weapon on the table and *why*. Was it because he believed he'd lost the battle? Or was he banking on my reluctance to harm an unarmed man, despite the havoc he'd wrought tonight?

"Civilized? You sent hired killers to my apartment," I reminded him.

"I had to do that. You're out of control." He pointed a finger at me. "I've never seen a clusterfuck of a mission like this in all the time I've been working as a handler. And the whole disaster is in your court, buddy."

This guy had all the brass of a classic narcissist, I thought.

"Look at you," he continued. "You roll into town like it's party city. Eat, drink, surf, repeat. What the fuck? You call that professional conduct? Did you even think about who might be trying to interfere with your assignment? You acted like a rookie, letting this one hook up with you. Worse than a rookie. Like a goddamn fifteen-year-old."

"Looks like *you've* got a party going on here, Vaughn."

"Don't you worry about that, buster. I'm operating completely within my rights. According to the Division Procedures Manual, Protocol Section M, item 12C, the operations facilitator—that's me—will liquidate and dispose of target assets in a timely and orderly manner, taking care not to create a negative historical disturbance."

"So, there's nothing in there about handlers plundering the treasury and enriching themselves."

"When is this going to sink into your thick skull? It's *my* business, not yours, dickhead."

I gestured vaguely at the surroundings. "I'd say this mission hasn't hurt you any. Volpe's yacht. His fortune. For all I know, you could have those teenage girls locked in one of these cabins. No, I'd say it looks like you're doing very well for yourself, in fact."

"Let me make this crystal clear, cowboy. I'm following protocol...by the book."

Avalie wandered toward the far side of the stateroom.

"Don't make yourself at home, surfer girl," Vaughn said, his voice dripping with sarcasm. "You aren't staying long."

"By the book?" I snapped. "You tried to kill us with poison gas in that shipping container."

"Maybe I did. But you were already off the rails," he said. "And did you even notice how I personally showed up to see with my own fucking eyes how you two were breaking all protocol at the beach?"

That day when he was watching me teach Avalie how to surf. He already knew her true identity by then, yet he kept silent about it.

Vaughn gestured towards Avalie. "That immobilizer of hers

was a dead giveaway. That was when I knew I had to get involved. It was my obligation to cut Division losses before the entire future of humankind went to shit."

I scoffed. "You don't care about the future. You've been undermining the mission from the start."

"Undermining the mission?" Vaughn barked a laugh. "This isn't about me, pal. This is all about you. This mission was doomed the minute you dropped into my time zone. You've broken every rule, every procedure."

Hearing him rant didn't mean a thing to me. I already knew what I had to do.

"What's the biggest worry the Division has? Section R, item 7, states that agents will avoid all contact with any ancestor or earlier version of themselves. What have you been doing? You've been cavorting all over San Clemente with your own mother. Your own *mother*!"

Vaughn was well aware of the formidable force the woman he was trying to recruit would become in the future. While persuading her to join him offered numerous advantages, he remained perfectly content even without her, thanks to Volpe's fortune.

"And this one. She comes in here, using an AI assistant that a five-year-old could have hacked into. Another breach of protocol. Good thing I snatched it. There's no telling what kind of Pandora's Box would have been blown open if the wrong people got hold of it."

The handler continued ticking off points as he directed his comments at me.

"But you want to talk about this mission? Face it, cowboy, you had the chance to take out your assigned target this afternoon, but you muffed it."

"As you like to say, Vaughn, that's my business. Not yours."

"Wrong. Read Section T, item 23. *The facilitator will intervene in the event of failure on the part of the agent to perform assigned duties.*

Failure? It's worse than failure. You fucked up big time. In fact, you've gone full rogue agent here. And this one..." He pointed at Avalie. "She's not only rogue. She's completely unauthorized. Section V, item—"

"Fuck those protocols," I snapped. "You tried to kill us twice. That's not intervention."

"You're a dangerous rogue operator. And this Mata Hari is the threat to all humanity." He pointed a finger at me. "I know what the Division wants, and it isn't you. They want agents who think with their heads, not with their dicks. So, get out of here. The two of you. When I make my report, you're toast. You hear me? Toast. And she's toast. The whole fucking lot of you are toast. So just tuck your tails between your legs and get out of here. You're done. You're finished."

He was pointing at the door, but neither of us moved.

"What are you gonna do?" he shouted. *"GET OUT OF HERE!"*

Pulling the bodyguard's pistol from my belt at the small of my back, I pointed the weapon directly between Vaughn's two surprised eyes and squeezed the trigger.

Chapter Twenty-Six

Avalie

Reed and I left the dinghy from the yacht on the beach next to San Clemente Pier and strolled past the silent restaurants and the deserted train station toward Avenida Victoria. The seaside town was sleeping at this late hour, its businesses shuttered.

I wasn't prepared to discuss what had transpired on that yacht with Vaughn. I didn't sense Reed was ready either. There were moments out there when I genuinely had no idea how things would unfold. Being a rookie, I wasn't familiar with the rules and citations Vaughn was rattling off. Still, I suspected there was some truth to what he said, albeit tinged with his own agenda.

"I'm going to miss this town," Reed murmured, casting a wistful glance around.

"Maybe they'll send you back and you get to see it again," I offered, trying to inject some optimism into the moment. I was glad he was changing the mood.

"Considering the mess we're leaving behind, and with no handler to clean it up, I suspect the Sheriff's Department has my face plastered on every corner."

"But maybe the news won't spread to other beach towns along the California coast," I mused. "Looking at the map, there are at least a dozen other places where you could do some serious damage."

"Hey, I didn't do all of that alone," Reed retorted with a half-smile.

I returned the smile, but inside, my chest tightened with the weight of unspoken worries. Reed and I had faced numerous challenges tonight, but I couldn't shake the knowledge that there was still unfinished business ahead.

Nadine. Judy. Layla. Me. And of course Xander. Too many lives and futures hung in the balance, depending on what choices Reed decided to make.

We'd been caught up in our actions of trying to stay alive and tying up loose ends, as Reed saw it. But when it came to what mattered most to me—the reason why I jumped back in time—I hadn't heard any commitment from him. And this made every muscle in my body tense, my heart heavy.

There were multiple times when he'd saved my life tonight, and there were a few moments when I did the same. But regardless of all that—never mind what I felt for him—what mattered now was my family.

"Do we need to arrange for a car to come and pick us up, or are they close enough that we can walk to the house?"

There was no point in taking another step or prolonging this. I turned and faced him. We were standing at the edge of a little park near the trolley stop.

I took a deep breath. Then, in one fleeting moment, memories of my time with him from this entire week washed over me, threatening to overwhelm me. What I felt for him was too deep. The bond we shared, the way we complemented each other, was fresh and raw and unlike anything I had ever experienced. In that brief moment, I realized that there would never be another Reed in my life.

"Nothing has changed," I whispered, my voice trembling with emotion. "I can't take you back to them unless I know."

"I get that. But by now, you *do* know. You *should* know." His words came explosively, shocking me. He leaned closer, his face mere inches away from mine. "Do you know what my options were when we faced Vaughn?"

"What were they?"

"I could have done nothing," he said. "Just walked away and let him live. Reset this week. Reset you. Reset him."

He placed both hands on my shoulders, his gaze penetrating mine.

"Regardless of what he said, all his threats would have disappeared in the blink of an eye. His authority would never have exceeded mine," he stressed. "But what did I do? I killed the man. Although he deserved it, I still killed an unarmed man. And do you know why?"

I took a deep breath, forcing myself to keep my emotions in check. I needed to give him the chance to explain, to express his feelings, to convince me that those who mattered to me would be safe, rather than leaving me to speculate.

"I want this new chance. I want Judy to blaze a new path for herself. I want Nadine and her husband to have the life they once had. I know and I accept that there will be complications. My life, my future as I know it, will be different, it could take a very different trajectory. But whatever happens, however things turn out, it's all worth it to me. Because having you in my life is everything. I don't want to lose you, Avalie."

I melted into his embrace, his arms wrapping around me with a reassuring strength, grounding me in the present moment. His lips brushed against my forehead tenderly, sending a wave of warmth through me. I tilted my head up, meeting his gaze, and our lips met in a soft, lingering kiss.

"You know," I whispered when we finally pulled away from each other, "the decision to bring you to the house is theirs, not mine. It's up to Xander and Nadine."

"I understand. And I hope they understand that I want to see my mother one more time," he said softly.

It hit me hard. I grasped his words with a clarity that stung. Despite this change in history, the uncertainty of Judy's illness loomed over him. There was no guarantee she would live to see Reed grow older, let alone be a constant presence in his life.

"I'll give them a call," I said.

He nodded and took a few steps away to afford me the privacy I needed. It wasn't surprising when Xander answered on the first ring. He recognized the number and had already texted me earlier that Judy was safe at their house.

"Are you alright?" he asked.

Before I could respond, the phone was evidently put on speaker, and Nadine's voice joined in, echoing the same concern.

"Yes, Reed and I are both fine," I reassured them.

"I'm guessing all those sirens down around the Pier Bowl had something to do with you two," Xander remarked.

"Guilty as charged," I admitted. "But it was necessary. How is Judy?"

I moved closer to Reed and put the phone on speaker. I knew he would want to hear the answer.

"Starved, thirsty, and weak since she arrived. As expected," Nadine put in. "But the questions haven't slowed down."

Judy chimed in from their end. "Think of it as the chance to work with the designer on the prototype." She paused. "The after-effects are too heavy. I can totally work on that, though."

I glanced at Reed's face and saw the smile there. He was

definitely a proud son. But he was also restless. With his hands tucked into his pockets, he moved away again, giving me space.

"Nadine. Can I ask you a question?"

She came on the line, only herself. "What is it?"

"Can we come to the house? Can I bring Reed there? I understand if you'd prefer not to," I added quickly. "I know Xander can make arrangements to have Judy meet Reed somewhere other than at your house and—"

"You've been with him all night," Nadine interrupted me. "Through all the danger. Do you trust him?"

I stared at Reed's back, and my heart went out to him. I understood what he was going through at this moment. Impatient to see his mother again, but also knowing that this meeting didn't hold any promises. Before tonight, the future was as he knew it and as he lived it. Now it was an unknown entity, filled with new adventures. But new dangers, as well.

At that moment, Reed turned around and our eyes met.

"Yes, I trust him," I told Nadine.

"Then bring him to the house. Xander is sending a car for you two."

Chapter Twenty-Seven

Reed

July 2079

As I stood on the corner of 5th and Broadway in the heart of Los Angeles, the neon lights painted the night in hues of electric blue and crimson. The city buzzed around me, a cacophony of voices and machines intermingling in the humidity. The aroma of street food wafted through the air, tantalizing my senses. The competing rhythm of music echoed from nearby clubs, the driving bass of the nearest one reverberating in my chest like a second heartbeat.

I checked the time for what felt like the hundredth time. I shifted nervously, scanning the crowd for her familiar figure.

She was late. No, I was early. I was so wound up to hear how she'd made out today that I couldn't wait around our apartment as she'd asked me to do. I had to come out here and greet her as she exited Division headquarters.

Erase Me

The holographic billboards overhead flickered and changed, casting wavering images on the pavement. I glanced up, momentarily captivated by the dazzling display, but my attention quickly returned to the door I knew she'd be coming out of.

Rules had been broken, and false statements were filed upon my return. My account of what happened in San Clemente in 2023 was unexceptional as far as the books were concerned. Del Volpe and Nadine Finley were taken care of. Vaughn, my handler, had gone rogue, and he too had to be eliminated. There was nothing in the report about Avalie, nothing about meeting Judy. I brought back Avalie's issued weapons and erased any record of her borrowing them. She'd never traveled back in time.

Officially, this last jump was no different than any other I'd made in my decade-long line of assignments as an Assassin in the Quantum Commuter Division.

This is what, as Avalie said, being part of the family of the founders of the company did for me. No one questioned any of it. My report was accepted as fact. Period.

And I had a new girlfriend. Avalie Briar had just finished her basic training. Tonight, I waited for her as she received her Division placement.

Both of us recognized the significance of this, particularly with regard to her future well-being, given that she shared Nadine's mutations. In this fresh iteration of time, my mother's cancer had been cured. Judy attributed this to her decision to place herself among the initial subjects in the laboratory time trials. The repetitive disassembly and reassembly of human matter played a crucial role in the treatment. However, Avalie was hesitant to be subjected to laboratory experimentation. She preferred to get involved in the active program. And now I wondered what sector.

Where an agent was placed within the organization wasn't

influenced by the individual's choice, background, or recommendations alone. Instead, the decision was meticulously determined after a process of heavy psychological and physical profiling. Every aspect of an agent's personality, aptitude, strengths, and weaknesses were scrutinized and analyzed to determine the best fit for their skills within the organization.

This rigorous procedure ensured that each member was assigned to a section where they could excel and contribute most effectively to the overarching goals of the Quantum Commuters. It was a system designed to maximize success, ensuring that the right person was in the right place at the right time, minimizing potential risks and optimizing mission outcomes.

Unfortunately, all of this meant that I had no control over the outcome. I knew how dangerous the jobs we did were, across the organization. No matter how prepared an agent was, the risks were always high.

And now, all I could do was wait.

Massaging the tension in my neck, I checked the time again. As the minutes stretched into what felt like an eternity, the activity in the street began to lessen. Still, I remained rooted to the spot, my eyes never straying far from the building door.

And then, like a mirage materializing from the depths of my longing, I saw her. She stepped out of the door and passed through the crowd. Her short dark hair caught the neon light, shimmering like gold. A smile tugged at the corners of my lips as she drew nearer, her presence filling the space between us like a promise fulfilled.

She reached out, her hand finding mine, and suddenly, everything else faded away. At that moment, there was only Avalie and the overwhelming certainty that no matter what the future held, we would face it together.

"I'm sorry it took so long," she said, her voice soft.

I shook my head, unable to contain the surge of emotion welling within me.

"It doesn't matter." I gathered her in my arms for a moment before letting go. "Tell me what happened."

"Got my assignment," she said, a twinkle shining in her eyes and the corners of her lips lifting. "I start specialized training next week."

"You're killing me. What is it?"

"Guess."

I tried to think of the least dangerous group among the commuters, but none of them satisfied me. Instead, I shifted my focus to Avalie's personality, to the courage she displayed in jumping back in time, facing unknown challenges, confronting me, and protecting her family.

"The Bodyguards," I finally said.

Her chin dropped into her chest for a moment, then she laughed. Her hearty, genuine laugh warmed my heart.

"You're so smart."

As we started walking away, my mother's message was the first one that reached us. As CEO of the company, Judy already had Avalie's results and was congratulating her. Nadine and Xander were next to reach out, their messages filled with pride and encouragement for their granddaughter's achievement. Also, they were reminding us of the family cookout at their house this coming weekend.

"You finally get to meet my parents," she told me. "They're arriving from Ireland tomorrow."

"And you get to meet my father and the twins," I replied.

As I had suspected would happen, my parents did divorce. My father remarried, only to divorce again. He always struggled with his marital choices, but his love for his children never wavered. Fortunately, my twin sisters remained a constant presence in my life. My brother pursued his passion for research, finding his greatest happiness there. All of them, including Judy, were invited to the cookout this weekend.

My mother's relationship with Nadine and Xander began fifty-six years ago, evolving from financial support and friendship into something akin to a family bond.

Upon our return from the adventure in San Clemente, Avalie and I were surprised to learn that there had been a few instances in our personal history where we'd actually crossed paths, thanks to the connection between my mother and Avalie's grandparents.

"What do you think will be my first assignment?" she asked as we started walking.

"I'll see if I can leverage my influence with the organization bosses to get us to travel together."

"I'm all for that," she said, her eyes gleaming. "So long as we can bring Payam."

"Hell, no. That piece of junk's capability is less than a parrot's."

Avalie wasn't ready to give up on her AI assistant. Living with her now, I was well aware of all the hours she was spending retraining its logic and personality.

"Payam will win you over. Give it time."

I placed a kiss on her temple. That piece of shit had betrayed her once. I was slow to forgive. "Let's get back to the jobs. What should we be looking for?"

"An undercover operation. We could pose as a couple, infiltrating a criminal organization."

"While the bodyguard protects their cover identity, the assassin gathers intelligence and eliminates key targets," I added.

"Cool. Or a rescue mission," she suggested.

"Because of the kidnapping of a prominent political figure," I added.

"The bodyguard focuses on securing the victim's safe

return," Avalie said excitedly. "The assassin tracks down the perpetrators and dismantles their operation."

"We could also undertake a mission...that requires us to race against time."

"That would be awesome. Kind of like we just did in San Clemente." She smiled. "By the way, are any of these jobs like Mr. and Mrs. Smith?"

I pulled her closer, embracing her tightly. "We're not just like Mr. and Mrs. Smith. We're better."

"Way better," she whispered, her lips meeting mine in a tender kiss.

Author's Note

Dear Readers,

We sincerely hope that you enjoyed reading *Erase Me,* the second book in our Quantum Commuter series. Many of you, captivated by the journey begun in our first book, wrote to us asking for Nadine and Xander's next chapter. It was your curiosity and enthusiasm that inspired us to write this novel.

For our first-time May McGoldrick/Jan Coffey readers, you might wonder why we ventured into the realm of time travel after years of weaving tales of historical romance, suspense thrillers, and Westerns. The answer lies in a deeply personal journey.

In early 2022, I (Nikoo) received the challenging diagnosis of metastatic breast cancer. This came nineteen years after my initial battle with the disease. As I navigate through treatment, a journey that will continue for the rest of my days, my husband Jim and I found solace and inspiration—as we always have—in our shared passion for storytelling.

During those pivotal early months, as we grappled with the weight of my prognosis, the seeds of this series took root in our

Author's Note

conversations. These books are centered around quantum commuters, individuals who happen to be dealing with terminal illnesses. The stories offer a unique exploration of life, time, and personal fulfillment. Much like their creators, these characters find solace and purpose through journeys into the past, extending their lives in unexpected ways.

In the first book, *Jane Austen CANNOT Marry*, we chose the mountain town of Elkhorn as the setting for the Colorado portion of this story. For those of you who have read our Nik James Westerns, you're familiar with the place. We thought it would be fun to revisit this silver boomtown a century and a half after the gunslinger Caleb Marlowe strode along those streets.

Jane Austen is one of our all-time favorite authors. We don't have to tell anyone that she is one of the most important writers of her time. Her name is as well-known and her stories are as familiar to us as any author writing in the English language. But it occurred to us that if Austen knew she would be dying at the age of 41, how might she have acted? Would she have written with the same passion? The same genius? And added to that knowledge, what if we gave her a chance to spend her last years in the arms of a man who loved her? We know that she never married, but what if she were given that opportunity? Would she choose security? Or a legacy of literary greatness?

If you haven't read it, we hope you will.

In response to your letters, Nadine and Xander return in our second book, set against the backdrop of present-day San Clemente. As recent transplants to Southern California, we couldn't resist sharing the charm of this coastal paradise with our readers.

Jim and I approach each day with gratitude, mindful of the fragility of life's moments. We cherish the connection we share with each of you, our cherished readers, who allow us the privi-

Author's Note

lege of entertaining and hopefully enriching your lives through our stories.

As authors, we have always written our stories for you, our beloved readers. If you enjoyed *Erase Me*, please leave a review online and tell a friend, tell two friends, tell many friends. And please visit us on our website - www.MayMcGoldrick.com - for the complete list of our books and for the chance to keep up with our cancer journey on my blog.

Also, stop by our online store (the link is on our website) for books, bargains, gifts, and merch. Of course, you might be wondering why we have this store...and why you should buy your books directly from us. First of all, you'll pay less for our books than you'd pay to Amazon and other retailers. Second, you can buy vintage collectible editions - rare hardcovers, original mass-market paperbacks, and box sets that you won't find anywhere else. Plus, it helps us. As authors, we don't have to wait for 60+ days for some online retailers to pay us. So, come on by!

Finally, if you haven't already done so, sign up for our newsletter and follow us on BookBub.

Thank you. Wishing you peace and health...always.

About the Author

USA Today Bestselling Authors Nikoo and Jim McGoldrick have crafted over fifty fast-paced, conflict-filled novels, along with two works of nonfiction, under the pseudonyms May McGoldrick, Jan Coffey, and Nik James.

These popular and prolific authors write historical romance, suspense, mystery, historical Westerns, and young adult novels. They are four-time Rita Award Finalists and the winners of numerous awards for their writing, including a Will Rogers Medallion for Traditional Westerns, the Daphne DeMaurier Award for Excellence, the *Romantic Times Magazine* Reviewers' Choice Award, three NJRW Golden Leaf Awards, two Holt Medallions, and the Connecticut Press Club Award for Best Fiction. Their work is included in the Popular Culture Library collection of the National Museum of Scotland.

- facebook.com/MayMcGoldrick
- x.com/MayMcGoldrick
- instagram.com/maymcgoldrick
- bookbub.com/authors/may-mcgoldrick